Tendin

Kim Delmar Cory

Royal Fireworks Press
Unionville, NY

Library of Congress Cataloging-in-Publication Data

Cory, Kim Delmar.
  Tending Ben's garden / Kim Delmar Cory.
      p. cm.
  Summary: In 1929, twelve-year-old Kate risks her life trying to keep a promise always to look after her gentle little
brother, Ben, who their destitute, widowed mother allowed to
be adopted by a wealthy family in an attempt to get the rest
of the family through the Depression.
  ISBN 978-0-88092-778-9 (pbk. : alk. paper)
  [1. Brothers and sisters--Fiction. 2. Depressions--1929--
Fiction. 3. Family life--Michigan--Fiction. 4. Gardening--
Fiction. 5. Poverty--Fiction. 6. Tramps--Fiction. 7. Michi-
gan--History--20th century--Fiction.] I. Title.
  PZ7.C8174Ten 2009
  [Fic]--dc22
                                                    2009032600

Royal Fireworks Press
First Avenue, PO Box 399
Unionville, NY 10988-0399
(845) 726-4444
FAX: (845) 726-3824
email: mail@rfwp.com
website: rfwp.com

ISBN: 978-0-88092-778-9

Printed and bound in the United States of America on acid-free, recycled
paper using vegetable-based inks and environmentally-friendly cover
coatings by the Royal Fireworks Printing Co. of Unionville, New York.

I dedicate this book to
my children, Amanda and Justin,

the "real" Kate and Ben who inspired
this story of stubborn sibling love.

"Life itself is the most wonderful fairy tale."
Hans Christian Anderson

Prologue

Spring 1929

Ben's amber ringlets shimmered like summer wheat tassels in a breeze.

He examined the maple tree above him. Watched the shiny broad leaves sway, heard them over through the sound of his brothers' laughter on the tire swing.

Filtering through the leaves, a ray of sun found, lost, found an old pine cone, setting it apart from the rest of the world in a dusty halo of gold.

Ben noticed it all. Barely three, Ben noticed everything of worth.

Kate dug deep, her blonde, bobbed hair bouncing as she created a mound of sandy significance in front of her.

"Ben Boy, you aren't helping." She thrust a garden trowel at him. "You asked me to play with you. Smooth this down until I tell you not to."

His chubby hands grappled with the thick metal trowel. He patted lightly at the mound.

Kate grabbed the trowel. "No, like this." She shaped the mound with hard even slaps before cramming the makeshift shovel back into his hand. He pounded at the sand. Kate huffed disgust at her baby brother's sand-shaping incompetence.

Leo sat down across from Kate in the sandbox.

"Who said you could play?" she demanded, shaping her mound with precision.

"Mama."

She tossed a metal bucket at him. "Then you have to fill that."

Leo wrenched the trowel from Ben's hand and started to dig. The baby's pale blue eyes filled, his bottom lip quivering as he watched his older brother dig with his little shovel. Shuddering a sigh from head to toe, Ben paused, then lightly patted the mound with his hand.

Kate glanced up and saw Leo with the trowel. "Give it back!" she hollered. "That's Ben's."

Yanking the trowel out of his hand, she whacked Leo across his red striped shoulder with it. Ben exploded with his baby belly laugh, Leo ran into the house crying, and Kate was called Katherine May and forced to stand in the corner after making her four brothers butter and jam sandwiches for lunch.

1

"Paris inspired" the *Good Housekeeping* magazine ad had stated. "Smart frocks for Junior Miss."

The blouse of heavy flat crepe for Junior Miss has overlapping tucks about the hips...skirt on bodice top, is pleated down the front...rose beige...Lucerne blue...or navy...

Kate had waivered for awhile before deciding on the Lucerne blue in her note to Papa. Whatever the shade of blue, it sounded French.

She'd added the chiffon nylons shown on the next page. If Papa was spending $16.75 on her dress, why not another $1.65 for her nylons?

It was for her birthday, after all.

Kate was sure Papa had bought her the dress for her birthday a few months ago.

Before he'd been killed by the crash.

So she searched everywhere on the farm she could think of. First closets. Then under beds. She knew he would have had to hide it from Mama and Mémère. They would think such a dress far too "mature" and costly for a twelve-year-old girl.

Especially these days.

Mémère thought the Devil hovered about women's knees anyway.

But Kate knew her Papa would have spent a hundred dollars on her if she'd wanted something that dear.

4

Because she was Papa's princess. Hadn't he told her that every day of her life? No matter how tired he seemed when he came home from the bank, Papa had always bowed to her ,and she'd curtsied to him. He'd kissed her hand, and she'd giggled as he followed it up her arm to tickle her neck, and lightly kiss each deep dimple.

She was his Princess Kate.

She had searched the barn, loft and all. Every outbuilding including the outhouse. She'd even volunteered to clean the chicken coop when it wasn't her turn, the nastiest job on the farm. But there was no package to be found.

Tommy had received a coveted aviator's cap like his hero, Charles Lindbergh, for his fourteenth birthday just a week ago. That had cost plenty, she was sure. Yet Mama had bought it for him. Kate had thought about stealing it and burying it in the old apple orchard. Had it all planned out. But then she thought Papa would probably have wanted him to have the cap.

Might as well have something Papa wanted come true.

"Katherine May."

Since Mémère spoke English instead of French today, Kate figured her grandmother must be in a good mood.

"Yes, Mémère."

Kate couldn't figure out how someone who prayed so much could look and act like one of Beelzebub's own. If she hadn't shared a bed with her, Kate would have suspected horns under the white braids coiled about her head and a tail beneath her floor-length black skirts.

"Gather the eggs for town." Mémère poked a scrawny finger at Kate, her shawl clamped about her hunched shoulders. "Break not one, please." Her small black eyes pinched her crinkled face like two June bugs.

"Yes, Mémère."

"Stop twisting your hair. It makes you look like a Baptist."

"Yes, Mémère."

Ben's Garden

Ben's garden consisted of a patch of dirt near the barn. Papa had dug it for him the previous year. How Ben had begged and cajoled for his very own garden to tend. Papa promised him seeds of his own to sow...beans, cucumbers, and melons. Potatoes, lettuce, and corn. Ben wanted sunflowers, so Kate stole some of the sunflower seeds Mémère liked to nibble when she tatted and mended.

Kate had helped Papa turn the soil and throw stinky manure fertilizer on Ben's garden last fall. This spring Kate alone had helped Ben hoe the soil, sow the seeds and water the rows.

Danced with him in the garden at dawn.

A bedraggled broom served as the body of Ben's scarecrow. Metal scraps from a rusty abandoned tractor in the orchard served as arms that whirled and clanked in the wind. Mémère gave him a shawl to drape about it. Using a shiny pie tin for the head, Ben painted the face with black tar. Circles for eyes, no nose. A wide grin that spanned most of the tin.

Tommy had warned Ben the scarecrow was supposed to be scary. To keep the crows, rabbits, and deer from eating his garden.

Ben had laughed. Thought that was silly. If the birds, bunnies, and deer wanted to eat from his garden, that was fine with him. That's why he had planted it.

He'd built the scarecrow for them to play with.

2

Friday, May 22, 1931

"Vern...," Mrs. Etta Crane smiled and motioned to a thin blond boy wearing short pants and a roomy green shirt, "could you please open the back door to invite a breeze?"

As the schoolroom quieted with a smattering of shushes, the hubbub of boys yelling and bats smacking baseballs grew louder through the open windows. Diminutive Mrs. Crane explained she would not be their teacher after this spring because her husband had finally found work in Detroit. And that monies earned from the sale of pies tonight would go towards keeping school open next fall.

Kate heard the words but didn't really understand them. Her focus had been on the doorway since she and Tommy had arrived half an hour earlier.

"Where's Tommy?" Margaret asked.

Mémère would think the Devil hovered around Margaret Vandervelde's knees tonight, Kate noted. Unfortunately, Mémère had assured that the Devil would remain a safe distance from Kate's knees when she had transformed Mama's mauve crepe dress for her. Yet Kate momentarily forgave Mémère her orneriness.

Because tonight Kate would not be wearing a dress sewn from a chicken feed sack.

"Tommy's outside," Kate answered. "Where's Harvey?"

She flattened the already flat mauve hair bow clipped to the back of her chin-length blonde hair. Tommy had told her

8

it looked like an airplane propeller on the back of her head. She'd bitten his pinkie finger. Drew blood.

"Harvey's coming later," Margaret said before setting her strawberry pie next to a sad looking apple pie, her name neatly scripted on the card beneath.

Evening in Paris perfume "borrowed" from Mama wafted from Kate's wrists. But the fragrance was waning. A sweat stream trickled down her back. She needed Harvey Vandervelde to walk through that doorway soon.

Pie-laden tables lined two of the four walls of the one room schoolhouse. In front of the other walls, parents and children sat in uneven rows of narrow wooden folding chairs. Men's dimpled fedoras and women's close fitting cloche hats fanned moist pink faces. Men were sweating while women glowed.

"What kind of pie did you bake?" Gracie Mortensen asked.

Spotting the other three Mortensen sisters throughout the crowd, each wearing chicken-feed-sack dresses that matched Gracie's, Kate couldn't help but swish her skirt as she spoke.

"My grandmother baked it."

Gracie's eyebrows arched.

"But I helped her," Kate lied.

"We'll start the bidding at 5 cents," Mr. Dekker announced, his resonant voice quieting the room.

"I've been meaning to stop by and pay my respects, dear."

There stood Mrs. Wagner, whose wide face appeared to be as red as her dress.

"Such a shame. Your father..."

"Thank you," Kate knew to say, even if she didn't mean it. She leaned to watch the doorway through the crowd.

9

"He wasn't the only one, of course," Mrs. Wagner continued, wiping her expansive brow with a lace handkerchief. "But to leave your mother and you children..." She sounded like she had swallowed an entire tin of Mr. Rademacher's homemade maple syrup. "Of course, many of our congregation pray for his soul to reach heaven."

Kate stared at the wide, red woman, who seemed to be the only one not moving in the room. She didn't make any sense. Papa had been killed by a crash when a Ford pick-up had hit him crossing Amsterdam Street. *Not the only one what? Nobody had been with him that day.*

Briar Rose was a princess who awoke after a hundred years of sleep when a handsome Prince kissed her echoed through her thoughts like a litany, as it seemed to do whenever someone spoke of Papa's accident.

Adjusting her feathered hat, wide, red Mrs. Wagner smiled a benevolent farewell before settling her girth tentatively onto a wobbling chair. Kate hoped for splinters.

"Kate!" Gracie yelled, then whispered, "Sam Kersten bought my pie for two dollars."

Listening to bids on pie after pie, Kate's gaze rarely left the open doorway, which showcased a pumpkin and gold sky. A welcome breeze stirred a blue flower print cotton curtain, and her bangs, as evening swallowed day. A unified sigh embraced the crowd with the cooling comfort.

She thought of Ben. She'd told him they couldn't say good night to the lake tonight. But tomorrow night they would stay all the longer, she'd promised. She'd smiled. He hadn't, his blue eyes huge with sadness.

Couple after couple sat sharing pies. Only a few pies remained. Including hers.

She heard Margaret call to him before she saw him.

Harvey Vandervelde. Seventeen and the loveliest, smartest, best dressed, most popular boy within a hundred miles, to

Kate's mind. One blond lock flitted across his forehead, eyes as blue as a midwinter sky flickered across the noisy room.

Hands stuffed deep within his trouser pockets, Harvey spoke briefly with his sister. He shook his head a few times as Margaret smiled. Sighing, Harvey turned and threw a weak "hello" smile Kate's way.

Kate thought she was breathing. Then again, maybe she wasn't. Sweat more than trickled down her back now. She swished for self assurance.

"Here's a fine peach pie created with tender loving care by Miss Kate Penton. Who bids 5 cents?"

Ten minutes later Kate's bottom barely touched the chair as she ate her peach pie with Harvey Vandervelde. Two dollars he'd bid and won. She wished it had been more than Sam Kersten had bid on Gracie's pie, but she was sitting next to Harvey Vandervelde. He had chosen her pie. And outbid at least three others to win it. He'd smiled at her. It didn't even matter that he had voted for Emma Karlstrom in the prettiest girl contest. Kate was sure it was only because their mothers were best friends.

Kate's heart thundered so she couldn't hear Tommy talking to her.

"We're leaving, Kate," Tommy repeated through a mouth full of stolen apple pie. "Let's go."

"What?" she asked, finally focusing on her brother.

"Let's go."

"But...I'm still eating my pie with Harvey," Kate announced while daintily nipping at a slice of peach on her fork.

Harvey's eyes met Margaret's across the emptying room.

"I can take Kate home," he offered.

Tommy shrugged, swiped one more mouthful of pie from a half empty tin, and left.

11

Kate walked through her front door at least an hour after her curfew. She fully expected Mama or Mémère or both to meet her with a switch.

Not that she cared.

Harvey had indeed driven her home. Along with Emma Karlstrom.

Kate was crammed in the back seat.

Emma and Harvey had shared the contents of a silver flask, singing "I Got Rhythm" loud enough to scare the feathers off Mrs. Wagner's hat. Along the way they stopped at telephone pole after telephone pole looking for bottles of homemade gin Harvey had stashed earlier. Evidently he couldn't recall which telephone poles he'd hidden the homemade hooch behind.

The evening only improved. When a staggering Harvey had told Kate to make sure to tell his sister that he had fulfilled his promise to her of showing Kate a good time at the pie social. And that now Margaret couldn't tell their parents about the gin still he and Robert Dykheusen had built in Robert's basement.

That's when he had kissed Emma. Who, Kate decided, despite her flowing blonde curls, had eyes too close together to have won the prettiest girl contest.

The screen door closed with a single muted thud. Kate sighed. Mama and Mémère sat at the dining room table. Any thought she might have had of sneaking through the parlor up to the bedroom had just disappeared like Ben's feet into a puddle.

Kate closed her eyes. And prepared herself.

Mama poured steaming tea into the pink and rose decorated china tea cups she had painted years ago before settling the teapot between herself and Mémère. She nodded at Kate.

Reminded her to wash before bed, to say her prayers, and bade her good night.

Splashing her face, Kate wondered. Mama hadn't said a word to her about coming home late. About letting an older boy drive her home.

And Mama and Mémère never stayed up past ten o'clock.

Kate donned her nightdress and tip-toed back down the stairs and across the wooden floorboards without a creak as she had learned to do through the years.

To eavesdrop from the parlor.

The Lake

"Why are there colors in the sky?" Ben asked, scanning the horizon, his high pitched five-year-old boy voice void of "r" and "s" sounds.

Resting the oars, Kate sat thoughtful for a moment, taking in the cottony layers of lavenders, golds and pinks above the trees, and reflected in the lake.

After chores, after dinner, after everything, she would find Ben, and they would say good night to the lake.

"Once upon a time," she began, "a giant ogre wandered this land. He was mean and ugly and ate children."

Ben stared at her with his usual enormous-blue-eyed intensity. As if she was the teller of all truths.

"Then, one day, a handsome prince with a magic sword slayed the ogre. And..." she shoved an oar into the water, "when he cut the ogre into tiny pieces, all the magic from his sword exploded into the sky." Kate's arms opened toward the darkening skies. "And the magic turned into beautiful colors that can only be seen this time of day."

"Why?"

"Because this was the time of day the magic happened."

She grabbed both oars, rowing toward shore in silence.

Ben examined the sunset, closing his eyes to resee it within his eyelids.

"I thought it was left over colors from rainbows," he lisped, eyes still closed. "Leftover water and sun and sky."

Kate tugged one last tug on the oars. She climbed out, pulling the boat onto shore.

"I like my story better."

She steadied the boat so Ben could step out. They hauled the rowboat into the brush, Ben's scrawny, scabbed legs

14

walking twice as fast, his thin arms lifting half as much as his sister's.

His slender fingers wiggled for Kate's hand.

"Me too."

3

Ben was gone.

He'd sat on Kate's lap in the front of the pickup truck, clutching his Green Turtle Cigar tin

She savored the sweet damp tendrils at the back of his neck.

His little boy smells of dirt, lemonade, and fresh green beans.

The square of tawny gold hair above his right ear.

She smoothed the blue checkered cloth holding the cornbread on her lap. She'd brought it for Ben, but he'd been too excited to eat. Too excited to go play with his "new friends" as Mama had explained it to him.

When Kate had overheard Mémère and Mama talking last night about losing the farm, and sending Ben away, Kate had bounded into the dining room, Mémère's tea cup halting mid-way to her prune lips. Kate had offered to stay at the Children's Home too. One less mouth to feed. And she could still take care of Ben.

It had taken her breath away, hearing Mama speak from a dark place Kate had never heard before, her soft voice turned deep and harsh, like a storm cloud speaking. Blaming Papa for all their money troubles.

The Children's Home had an opening, and she was lucky to have Ben accepted there.

Ben would be better off, Mama had said, where he could have plenty to eat. Kate had to bite her tongue when she'd

16

heard that. Ben ate less than a bird. The twins, Leo and Raymond, rivaled the pigs when they ate.

Kate was needed at the farm to help prepare for the auction the bank would hold, Mama had said. Where the house, barn, and even the clothes on their backs could be sold to anyone who bid on them to pay the bank note.

Kate had asked when Ben would be coming home. Mama had said that would be worked out in time. She poured Mémère more tea and told Kate to go to bed.

Half an hour ago they'd left Ben playing with a big red fire truck with a ladder that really worked in the playroom of the Children's Home outside of town. Mama told him to be a good boy, to play nicely with his new friends, and they would be back for him. As Kate had walked toward the door, Mama's arm latched onto hers mostly to keep her from returning to Ben. He had come running. Begged Kate to stay and play with him. Unable to look him in the eye, she'd laughed falsely and said he would have more fun playing without her.

But she'd be back for him. She promised. That had made Ben smile.

"Can we dance in my garden?" Ben asked, giggling, fiddling with Kate's fingers.

"Yes, Ben Boy."

Staring out the truck window at fields and road that united into one dry, brown, flat forever, Kate thought the landscape reflected her feelings. She'd spent last night at the pie social with that stupid Harvey Vandervelde instead of saying good night to the lake with her Ben.

She'd always promised Ben that they would run away together. Live in a castle together. That she'd always take care of him.

Now he was gone. And she remained. Alone. No Papa. No Ben.

Her mother's sniffling into a hankie interrupted Kate's thoughts. The white lace collar her mother wore flopped unevenly like a dying bird's wings against her grey silk dress with every road rut and bump. Nestled into her door, Kate examined her mother. Dressing so fine for the occasion of casting off her youngest like a sack of spoiled potatoes. Kate created as much distance between herself and her mother within the truck cab as between the moon and sun.

A rushing roar plugged Kate's ears. Heat throttled her throat; her head ached like a thousand rocks had been piled upon it. As punishment. For letting Ben go.

Her heart no longer beat. It weighed like an anchor, pulling her down. Heavy and still. Silent. Mémère would be pleased, thought Kate, that she felt such a penance.

She closed her eyes to see Ben again. Sitting in their rowboat. On their lake. "How do birds fly?" she heard his small lisp.

She wouldn't cry. Mama had no tolerance for tears. Kate had witnessed that at Papa's funeral.

Her shaking hand struggled to crank her window all the way down.

"Katherine, please roll that back up," her mother demanded, masking her face from the dust clouds with her handkerchief.

Kate thought that a more honest use of her embroidered hankie.

Unfolding the napkin on her lap, Kate scooped up the square of crumbly cornbread with both hands. Her mother's ocean blue eyes glowed cool against dark hair and fair skin as she stared at Kate over the top of her handkerchief. Kate refused them.

And scattered the bread out the window.

"Kate!" her mother screamed.

"What?" Tommy yelled, glancing several times at his mother, the truck zig zagging.

"Nothing," said Kate. "Keep driving."

"Katherine, you know perfectly well we are in no position to waste food. One of your brothers might well have eaten that."

This time Kate's eyes met her mother's. "It was Ben's bread."

Kate shook the remaining cornbread crumbs out the window, smiling small.

Ben would rather share his bread with birds than his brothers any day.

Green Turtle Cigar Tin

Ben thought it the finest box he'd ever seen.

There it was, crammed in the top of Mama and Papa's closet one day when he was helping Papa look for a certain hat.

Papa always said that Ben was his best helper.

Papa wore hats well, fedoras in the winter and skimmers in the summer, and he had an abundance of them. When Ben spotted the green turtle on the tin, he could hardly speak. Barely four at the time, he'd asked Papa in an awed whisper what that box might be. Papa had chuckled and said he'd had it from his cigar smoking days. He couldn't even recall what he kept in it now.

Ben jumped up and down in little Ben jumps, his small clapping hands like a hummingbird's wings, his eyes growing larger than Mémère's balls of yarn.

Papa emptied the tin with no apparent thought to its paper contents before handing it to his youngest son.

The rectangular tin was the size of a large lunch box, with a metal handle on the top and a thin metal clip that latched neatly onto a tiny knob on the front. Grass green served as the background, the wording and decorations vanilla in color. It showed a huge green turtle sitting on a rock, fluffy clouds lining the horizon. Flowers blossomed at the base; a delicate vine encircled the images. Six tiny holes had been punched into the bottom.

"Green Turtle" was neatly scribed above the turtle, "Cigars" below. A smoking stogie steamed from the turtle's mouth.

It might have been a gift from the Magi the way Ben accepted it with open-palmed grace.

From that day on, Ben was rarely seen without the Green Turtle Cigar tin. He stashed his treasures in it; leaves, twigs, a bladeless straight razor Papa had given him.

Ben could be heard before he was seen by the gentle squeaking of the handle on his Green Turtle Cigar tin.

Ben Gone 8 Days
Sunday, May 31, 1931

The day started before dawn.

The twins fed the horses, Carlos and Mr. Big, and readied them to spend most of the day in the pasture. Tommy and Kate milked Daisy, Bony Girl, and Nona and separated the cream from the milk. Next they fed the chickens, gathered eggs, and slopped Henrietta and Pegasus.

Kate didn't sing and dance when she fed the chickens the way Ben did. She couldn't call them by name as he did. She just scattered the seed and wondered if the ugly creatures knew the difference. Likely they did, she thought.

After breakfast each morning, everyone worked in the family garden, which had doubled in size since last year. Mama planned on selling vegetables at a roadside stand this summer. They had added asparagus and rhubarb along the side of the garden as well as berry bushes. Anything to create an income, Mama had decreed.

Once a sunshine yellow farmhouse had peaked through the fir trees of their winding drive. Not anymore. Yellow was but a memory, the paint weathered to the color of Lake Michigan sand in splashes across the four bedroom house. The yellow paint Papa had bought a few years ago could be spotted in the barn next to the rusting plow harness.

Originally their plow horse, Irish Boy, had helped dig the long narrow furrows in the almost barn-sized garden between the house and the woods. He was sold about a month after Papa died. Papa had been working on fixing their tractor. Since the twins were born. Seeds had been ordered and paid for the fall before. Mama said that was the only thing that had gone right in a year.

Every few weeks they sowed new seeds depending on their season. Celery, beans, cabbage, carrots, and peas were planted in April. Mid May saw lettuce, onions, muskmelons, tomatoes, and watermelon seeds in the ground. In late May they usually planted a crop of spinach, potatoes, celery, corn, lettuce, and onions to mature for winter use.

Papa had plans of reworking the run-down apple orchard across the field behind the house. He'd said that's why he had purchased the farm right after Tommy was born. He'd bought books on running orchards. Said when the time was right, he would quit his job at the bank and run the apple orchard. Maybe open a bakery, sell the house, and move into town. Mama had always wanted to live in town.

But what had been twenty acres when he bought the farm had become fifteen acres. Then twelve. Eight acres now supported the farm, pasture and orchard after Papa had sold it off, acre by acre over the years, for money to invest in "a sure thing."

Papa had bought the gardening books; Mama had figured it all out. She'd even drawn a garden plan with the rows. Labeled each with the vegetable and the date of planting in her fine handwriting that flowed and curved like a flower. Kate knew Mama used to paint flowers on tea cups for pleasure and pride.

Once upon a time.

Kate expected Ben had inherited her artistic nature.

After supper and chores every evening since Ben had been sent away, Kate worked in his garden.

The sky transformed from light blue to amber and pink. To sapphire. The lake called to her. But she couldn't go. Not without her Ben. Instead she hoed and weeded and watered.

Mama insisted everyone focus on preparing for auction day. The bankers would come to inventory the property and its contents. They wanted to make sure nothing was hidden before the auction.

The men in suits wanted their money.

Tommy, Ben, and Papa had built the wooden bird house that had hung off the parlor side of the wraparound porch last summer. Ben had handed the nails to Tommy, who hammered them as Papa held the wood in place.

Ben's goat, Pancake, ate everything that crossed his path. Including weeds, cereal boxes, and Mama's favorite blouse off the clothesline.

Neither the birdhouse nor Pancake would be found on auction day.

Ben Hums and Draws

Kate couldn't carry a tune in a basket, but Ben could sing true. He hummed while playing with bugs or feeding Pancake. He hummed while chasing butterflies. Or drawing.

Ben could take any scratch of pencil on a piece of paper, or mark in the dirt, and make it into an animal or flower or bird drawing. Once he turned a scratch in the ground into a magnificent flying bird, spread wings and all. Kate built a stick fence around it so no animals or twins would ruin it. The rain erased it after a few days.

5

I'll wear Ben's favorite dress, Kate thought.

She had used money gained from selling the pharmacist empty medicine bottles found behind Dr. Smythe's office to buy drawing papers and a sketching pencil for Ben. Along with a licorice whip. She stored them in the purple and gold silk purse Papa had bought for her ninth birthday. Lined in plush purple velvet, it was fit for a princess, Papa had said.

Tommy had bought a copy of *The Detective Hour* magazine for himself.

Thus they shared an unspoken promise of secrecy.

Mama insisted on receiving every penny earned within the family. Kate listened nightly from her bed to the uneven click and scrape of coins as Mama counted and then tried to place them silently in the elf cookie jar that scared Ben so.

The grippe had struck, postponing the auction until after the Fourth of July holiday. Mama forbade anybody to travel to town for two weeks. Stores closed. Father St. Denis even cancelled Mass for two weeks running. People walked about with handkerchiefs over their mouths for protection from the coughing, fever, and stomach ills running rampant.

Mama had run out of coffee, sugar, and flour. No bread could be baked. When Mrs. Timmons visited one afternoon, calling from her automobile first to ask if the grippe had reached them, she brought a lovely lemon cake.

It was devoured before the dust had settled behind her Model T.

Muttering under her breath, a sneer causing her dry, thin lips to all but disappear as she sipped her tea, Mrs. Timmons had revealed how the out-of-work and homeless people milled outside the now closed library where they usually spent their days. Some of the soup and bread lines had closed also.

She didn't care for this, she shared in a whisper, her lips disappearing completely. When these places in town closed, she explained, it tended to send "those people" outside of town to beg for food. To *their* farms.

Mrs. Timmons informed them that the Children's Home was under quarantine, several children having taken ill. Mama had said she was sure Ben was fine. Kate wondered how she could know, since their telephone had been disconnected for three weeks. Nobody had been by the farm since then.

Kate begged Tommy to drive her to the Children's Home, but he said he couldn't. No gas for the truck. Smiling, he told her she could ride Mr. Big into town, knowing since the twenty-hand's-high horse had kicked her in the backside last year, she would have nothing to do with riding him or any other horse.

She wanted to ride Tommy's bicycle into town, but he had a flat tire and wouldn't fix it, claiming he had too many chores to do. So for the entire two weeks, Kate behaved, hoping her angelic demeanor would result in gaining permission to visit Ben.

She and her brothers worked from dawn until dusk gardening, canning, and selling fruits, vegetables and eggs at their rickety roadside stand on dusty silver-skied days when even the thought of a breeze would be welcomed. Precious few people drove by with so many already ill or afraid of catching the grippe. Then it was back to evening chores and preparing a meatless, breadless supper. Mama made lots of vegetable soups.

Evenings, when others were readying for bed around 8:30, Kate focused on Ben's garden. She wanted his garden ready for him when he came home.

When word came that most quarantines had been lifted, Kate decided no matter what Mama or anyone else said, she was bringing Ben home. She'd sneak him out if she had to. Once he was home, she was sure they wouldn't want to send him away again.

His empty seat at the dinner table plucked so at her heart.

Ben needed her. Nobody understood that he spoke only when it suited him. That he needed to be near trees and sky and bugs. His lake. That he needed to draw as much as he needed to breathe. Everywhere she looked, on the farm was where Ben needed to be.

Tommy sat in Papa's chair now. It hadn't happened right away. Just one day, Kate looked up and there sat Tommy at the head of the dining room table.

One day he had been a boy, the next a man.

Mama no longer went into town for shame of buying on credit, although she wouldn't admit to it. She claimed she was too busy canning. Tommy and Kate now took care of selling the eggs, cream, and vegetables to buy gasoline, food, and supplies at Carlstrom's Mercantile.

Kate smiled.

Her mother's prideful nature would help Kate bring Ben home.

Ben and the Doctor

Once when Ben was about a year old, Doctor Smythe had been called to the house because Ben croaked like a bull frog when he coughed. Ben wouldn't open his mouth for the doctor to look down his throat. Until Kate told him to. Then Ben cried, and Kate cried harder and kept crying until long after Ben had stopped.

6

Ben Gone 32 Days
Wednesday, June 24, 1931

After finishing their errands, Kate made Tommy drive towards the edge of town. The line of men, women, and children snaked around for a block or more now that the soup kitchens had reopened. She had heard Mama say their own family wasn't far from standing in these lines. Begging. Thanks to Papa.

As if Papa had wanted to be killed by the crash, thought Kate.

An automobile passed them, and Tommy steered almost off the road, forcing Kate to brace herself against the dusty dashboard.

"Why don't you want to see Ben?" she asked above the roar and clank of the truck.

Tommy glanced at her in silence.

"Don't you miss him?"

"Of course I miss him," Tommy erupted. "He's my brother. He's...Ben."

Three scant bags of groceries barely filled a corner of the Model T's cargo bed. Sun slanted amidst lush green maple leaves above the dirt road. Slivers of light bounced, dappling the road in an uneven rhythm. A road song, Ben would have declared before sharing his version of it.

Soon, she told herself, they would be singing together again in Ben's garden.

As Tommy approached the white clapboard Children's Home, Kate jumped out of the cab. They were expected home shortly. Tommy lingered, saying he needed to check something on the truck. Kate didn't take the time to argue with him.

"Don't take long," he warned.

She hadn't informed Tommy of her plans to bring Ben home with them today. He didn't need the added responsibility, she told herself. Ben would be home for the Fourth of July holiday. How he loved the fireworks, plugging his ears, humming as he watched. They always went in town and watched a movie that was shown outside for free against the pharmacy wall, and they ate store-bought ice cream. At least they had when Papa was alive.

Mémère's gold pocket watch could almost be heard ticking from the farm. How could Mama be angry at them for being late if Ben was with them?

Groups of children played on the front lawn of the children's home. Girls wearing matching chicken feed and flour sack dresses scattered jacks, skipped hopscotch squares and jumped rope while boys pitched baseballs and clicked marbles. Two young boys in short pants and suspenders like Ben wore swung hard on a tire swing. Kate realized there were fewer children playing than when they had first brought Ben thirty-two days ago. Her eyes narrowed, searching. She listened through the bickering and laughter. No Ben.

They would have eaten supper by now. Kate tightened her grip on the silk bag slung across the front of her dress. Maybe Ben was inside doing chores. He'd always helped clear the table at home. She pictured him, careful as he always was, clearing plates to the sink. One by one. Heard his sweet soft humming of no song in particular.

The wide front door sat propped open on this late June afternoon.

Kate worked her way counterpoint through four boys running out the doors. She looked about the entryway with its worn, elegant rugs and heavy, dark furniture. The only hint of illness appeared to be several cots stacked in a corner under folded green blankets.

Almost sprinting, Kate passed a sparrow-like young woman with short, wavy brown hair and a white apron over a knee length cotton dress. Kate thought the brown dress lovely in its own way, but hardly as stylish as the Lucerne blue birthday dress of her dreams.

"May I help you?" the woman asked, her fingers lighting on Kate's arm, her grey eyes intense with concern. "You shouldn't be here."

Kate skidded to a stop. "My brother," she said, almost breathless, sweat slipping down the side of her face. "I came to get him."

"We've just lifted the quarantine, but..."

The woman looked tired, Kate noticed. Her already small face thin and sallow.

She lifted a chart hanging from a row of hallway hooks. "What's your brother's name?"

"Ben Penton," Kate huffed, glaring at the grandfather clock gracing the back wall.

Upon reviewing the chart, the sparrow-like woman hailed a tall woman wearing a lavender dress with tiny white polka dots. She shared the chart. The polka dot woman looked at Kate.

Kate recognized that look.

Like Mrs. Wagner.

Smoothing the skirt of her flour sack dress, Kate focused on one tiny pink sprig. Ben liked this dress because it reminded him of the flowers by the lake.

"Come with me, my dear," the polka dot lady said softly.

Kate's jaw clenched. She thought she heard Ben's belly laugh in the distance.

Ben.

"We've come to take my brother home," Kate said as best she could without breathing, as she followed the woman into a sheltered area.

"My dear...what is your name?"

Kate glanced at the clock. "Kate Penton. My brother is Ben Penton. I haven't seen him in thirty-two days. We've come to take...him home." She stroked her silk bag.

Ben, I brought you drawing papers and a pencil.

The woman sighed, touching Kate's hand as though it might break. "I was sure you would have been told."

Briar Rose was a princess who awoke after a hundred years of sleep when a handsome Prince kissed her.

Tommy shadowed the hallway. Kate stared at the polka dot lady as if she were a snow-laden tree in August.

"Ben is no longer with us."

The purple and gold silk princess bag with Ben's drawing papers, pencil and licorice whip lay crumpled on Kate's lap. She smoothed it for the paper's sake, a single golden thread unraveling with her touch.

She hadn't spoken for twenty minutes. Neither had Tommy.

"You knew, didn't you?" She whispered the accusation in a small un-Kate like voice.

She hadn't looked at her brother since climbing into the truck. Without Ben.

"Why did you let me...?"

"I...just...I didn't know how to say it."

Her stare bore hard into his profile. Mama's dark hair, Papa's strong nose and chin.

"They...Samuelsons own the Ford dealership in town. They lost a little boy about Ben's age a year ago. Smallpox. They took in Ben and two sisters from the Children's Home during the grippe for safekeeping. The girls returned..."

"But they didn't give Ben back?" Kate asked in a huff.

"Mama thought he would be...better off for now."

Kate willed the truck to speed up and stop simultaneously.

"So they want Ben to replace their son?" Kate screamed, almost standing in the truck cab. "He belongs with *me*! They can't have him!"

"Sit down, you'll..."

The truck door flew open as Tommy slowed to a stop in front of the house.

"Mama!"

Kate thundered across the porch, the screen door slamming hard behind.

Magnifying Glass

Summer 1930

"What are they doing?" Tommy asked, resting against the fence he was repairing, gulping cool water Kate had brought him. "Playing marbles?

Shading her eyes with one hand, she focused in on the twins, who hovered over the ground by the garden. A glint of summer sun scampered across the side of the barn. Tommy's hammering disrupted the afternoon calm.

"Those nasty, stupid..." she ranted.

By the time she reached them, it was too late.

Ben wailed and thrashed an hysterical Leo while Raymond braced Ben with one hand. Leo held a small magnifying glass over a smattering of black specks.

"That's Ben's, and you know it!" Kate screamed, grappling for the glass.

"Here, you can have the stupid thing," Raymond finally spit, dashing it into the dust. He'd grabbed a recovering Leo, and they'd laughed and shoved each other all the way to the house.

Sniffling, Ben plopped next to the fried ants. He whispered to them. His splattering tears might have revived them with tender hope. But they didn't. Bit by bit, he scooped beneath them until they all lay within his open palms.

He looked at Kate through glistening blue eyes, and she knew what would happen next. What always happened if a butterfly or beetle or bird died within a mile of Ben.

The ceremony by the lake at dim of day was followed by Ben singing a "Goodbye Ants" hymn in his wonderfully true, little boy voice.

That night Raymond didn't have to guess how Mémère's urine soaked sheets ended up stuffed in the foot of his bed.

7

Ben Gone 34 Days.
Friday, June 26, 1931

Kate had confronted Mama on Wednesday, but Mama had refused to "discuss the matter" with her. Said Kate would come to understand in time.

Ben wasn't a "matter." He was Ben. Her Ben.

What would Papa say if he knew Mama had tossed Ben away like a loaf of moldy bread? Let complete strangers tend to him?

Kate needed to find her dress. Papa would want her to find it, she knew.

First she looked in all the places she had looked before. Just in case she might have missed something.

Everything in the barn had been turned topsy turvy as they prepared for the auction. Surely a package containing her dress wouldn't have been thrown out accidentally. She didn't take any chances. Halfway through mucking out Irish Boy's stall, it hit her.

The corn crib.

Snagging her work dress on a nail as she threw her rake down, Kate ran to the wooden structure next to the barn, where corn was stored to feed the animals.

Since the corn only came to her knees, she decided all she needed to do was hop in and walk about the musty corn cobs to be able to feel a package beneath. She trotted in circles, starting near the walls and working her way clockwise, then counterclockwise toward the center. Her only discovery was that her torn chicken feed sack dress was now stained with mold and dirt around the hem.

Inspiring her all the more to find her new birthday dress.

After revisiting the chicken coop, outhouse, kitchen and parlor, she decided to explore the bedroom she shared with Mémère.

If Mémère had found her dress in their room, Kate certainly would have heard about it. In French or English or both. Along with several assigned Hail Marys.

Papa was clever, though. He would have hidden it so Mémère would never find it.

While Mémère rocked, tatted, and sniffed snuff on the front porch, Kate investigated their bedroom. Her biggest challenge was the large steamer trunk where Mémère kept her wedding dress and other ancient treasures. After rummaging through the trunk, closet, and under the bed, Kate decided Papa couldn't have known she would have to look for her own birthday dress. It wasn't his fault she couldn't find it.

Sitting on the bottom stair between the dining room and parlor, legs tucked so neither Mama nor Mémère could see her torn, soiled skirt, she could well imagine how Papa had anticipated the look of pure joy on her face when she opened the beautifully wrapped box. Probably yards of fine lace ribbon tied in a giant bow. Pink. Yes, he would have wrapped it in pink, she was sure.

For a moment she thought about making Tommy join her in her search. After all, he'd received his aviator's cap for his birthday. It was only fair he help her find her birthday dress.

Deciding against enlisting Tommy's help, Kate was about to search the twins' room when Mama found her and made her take laundry off the clothesline.

She stayed busy until long after dinner with chores, but placed Leo's clean folded clothes in Raymond's dresser drawer and vice versa. Just because.

How Ben Eats

While the twins attacked their fried chicken and mashed potatoes with all the manners of hungry wolves devouring fresh kill, Ben sat.

"Ben," his mother said in her 'this-is-the-last-time-I'm-going-to-say-this' voice. "You will eat what's put in front of you or go hungry."

Mémère spoke French to Ben. Then English. "Eat, Benoit. There is none to waste."

"Can I have his?" Raymond managed through stuffed cheeks, losing a spurt of potato with his effort.

Kate watched in silence. Never had Ben eaten meat. Yet they kept trying to make him. Now that meat was rarely served, it seemed all the more important to them that he eat it.

But he wouldn't. He never gave a reason. Ben wasn't one to speak unless he thought it important. He didn't find his not eating meat important.

He just didn't.

"Eat your potatoes, Ben Boy," Kate urged in a hush.

Her mother eyed Kate with open-mouthed disdain and excused Ben from the dinner table. Raymond almost swallowed Ben's chicken whole while Kate sneaked cornbread and cold potatoes to Ben after bedtime.

8

When Mrs. Van Dam arrived around eight that morning carrying a purple basket filled with steaming blueberry muffins, Kate had been up for three hours.

Half an hour later the Dortmeisters appeared bearing a fragrant cherry pie. Leo would have swiped it had Kate not shoved it into the kitchen larder.

Every half an hour or so, neighbors came into view through the trees lining the drive, rural angels in pick-up trucks, horse-drawn buggies and rumbling wooden wagons.

Mama had told Kate to make sure the twins wore clean clothes, especially Raymond. Kate couldn't see what difference it would make how Raymond smelled. People weren't here to bid on him.

After opening the bedroom curtains and thwonking Raymond on the head around 5:30, she had sniffed a folded shirt before tossing it at him. She'd instructed him not to wear it until after he'd finished his morning chores.

Raymond had just rolled over in bed. The second smack had him washing his face within seconds.

Leo jolted upright when he heard the floor boards creaking towards his bed.

Dressed in her summer best, Mama wore a soft green shift with a white lace collar and her grandmother's pearls. Her wavy black hair shone as brightly as her welcoming smile.

Kate wondered, had she found her birthday dress, might she have worn it today? She decided she wouldn't have.

It seemed stupid to Kate that Mama would dress so fine and smile so wide on the day she was losing everything she owned. Who was she trying to impress?

Closing her eyes, Kate spread her arms, swayed and sighed. She was Wendy, flying away to Neverland.

In a stunning Lucerne blue dress, Ben at her side.

By noon the thermometer mercury lingered at a steamy 92 degrees.

Almost a hundred neighbors and strangers mingled and chatted by the time the auction began at 1:00. The men in black suits had arrived around 10:00. They spent most of their time in the barn tagging equipment and setting up their tables for the bidding. That was fine with Kate, as she wasn't about to let them have one slice of pie or one glass of cold lemonade.

The kitchen smelled like a restaurant with Pyrex dishes of various sizes offering noodle casseroles, wicker baskets brimming with fragrant sweet breads, still warm fried chicken, and a rainbow assortment of lattice topped fruit pies and frosted cakes lining the counter.

Several women supervised the kitchen, cutting, serving, and cleaning while the other wives fretted over Mama. Mémère mumbled in French and rocked on the front porch, reminiscent of a rickety rowboat about to capsize. Her snuff box at the ready in the deep pocket of her long skirt.

The men stood on and around their vehicles, fanning hats for a breeze, smoking, spitting, and talking in low, tense voices. Wives brought them sweaty glasses of lemonade, wiping their hands on their aprons as they walked back to the house. Kate had put the twins to work squeezing lemons brought by Mrs. Wagner.

12:58 P.M.

"Ladies and gentlemen," sang the tall bespeckled man of the black suit, vest and hair.

Kate wished he might melt into a hot black puddle which she would immediately fill with pig slop. And call "pig, pig, pig" to award Henrietta and Pegasus a hearty last supper.

All the barnyard animals and farm equipment had been staged in and around the barn. The household items had been organized in the parlor and dining room.

Including the tea set Mama had hand-painted so many years ago, whose pink and yellow roses one could almost smell, showcased in the middle of the dining room table so it would surely be noticed by bidders.

It began with Mr. Van Ark, the pharmacist.

When the auctioneer started the bid on Papa's tractor at 5 cents, Mr. Van Ark bid one penny.

The auctioneer stopped, looked at him crossly, repeating the starting bid at 5 cents.

A man Kate didn't recognize bid 10 cents.

Mr. Vandervelde and two other neighbors sidled next to the stranger. When another man upped his bid to 12 cents, three neighbor men moved next to him.

Then Mr. Dykheusen bid one penny.

And so it went for the next two hours. If someone bid over a penny on anything, neighbors kindly requested that the person refrain from doing so. On more than one occasion, men were forcibly removed from the bidding process, ushered to their vehicles and "asked" to leave.

Kate knew it was more than the heat that created the wet darkness under the arms and down the backs of the auctioneer and bankers.

By the time the auction closed, proceeds for the bank totaled $7.35 instead of the hundreds of dollars the bankers had expected. The bank had to accept these monies as payment for what Papa owed on the farm.

All that had been bought, including the land and house, was returned to Mama by the neighbors who had made the purchases.

Including her hand-painted pink and yellow rose tea set.

Raymond Stinks

Kate figured Raymond smelled the way the Devil must look.

Tommy said he smelled like a swamp in July.

On laundry day, Kate hung Raymond's clothes where the sun would hit them the longest. At the opposite end of the clothesline from Ben's clothes. For some reason, Raymond's overalls didn't smell as bad as his shirts and pants.

Which Mama burned once they were outgrown.

Kate wondered if his size had anything to do with his stink. He was a good foot taller and twenty pounds heavier than his twin Leo. They really didn't look much alike, Raymond's red hair and freckles so different from Leo's dark hair and protruding ears.

On Saturday nights Kate bathed Ben in the kitchen sink when he was a baby. She just couldn't put him in that swirling black water in the upstairs tub after Leo and Tommy.

Raymond.

Not her sweet baby.

As Ben grew, Kate came to prefer using the large tin apple basin in the kitchen. She'd fix a bath just for the two of them.

Ben always last because sometimes he peed in it.

9

Kate stayed awake twisting her hair into knots the size of bumble bees the night after the Milos family arrived.

She had been helping Mama and Mémère make strawberry jam, sweat pouring out of her like gin out of Robert Dykheusen's still as she stirred the big black kettle on the blue enamel stove. Stopping once to listen, she wanted to shush Mama and Mémère but knew better. She was sure she heard something. They chatted in French about neighbors and dinner. Kate could understand that much.

All three paused this time.

A tiny rap, rap at the back porch screen door.

Mama's glance told Kate to check it as she and Mémère resumed their chatter. Kate swiped her forehead with her apron hem.

Stepping into the screened porch, Kate thought at first whoever had knocked had left. A breeze floated over her with what would have seemed steamy July air had she not just come from the bubbling, boiling heat of the canning in the kitchen.

She sighed and closed her eyes, allowing the cool to sprinkle over her like fairy dust. Or how she imagined fairy dust might feel. She wondered if when she opened her eyes she would be a sparkling princess.

Opening one eye, she saw she still wore a baggy chicken feed sack dress that Mémère had hemmed mid calf so she could "grow into it."

45

A chaos of dark curls peeked above the bottom half of the screen door.

The rap started, then stopped. Kate stepped closer. Coffee brown eyes within the face of an angel stared at her from beneath the curls.

"Katherine," Mama called from the kitchen. "Who is it?"

Smiling, Kate creaked the door open to invite the cherub inside.

"Could you kindly spare us a cup of water, Miss?" the angel whispered.

Confused by the plural, Kate scanned the yard. There they stood. In the shade of the black walnut and maple trees, between the gardens and the barn. The windmill well only a few yards away. A man and two children, a woman cradling an infant.

"Of course," Kate said, stooping to the girl's height as she spoke. Kate figured she couldn't be much older than Ben. "There's a cup hanging from the well."

By now Mama had joined her, wiping her hands with a tea towel. She smiled at the child.

The angel said, "Papa said we had to ask first," before her oversized yellow dress billowed like a picnic tablecloth with her curtsy. "Thank you, Ma'am."

She half ran, half skipped back to her family sharing the shade. The man removed his hat in deference to Mama before ushering his family towards the well. Kate would have watched them had Mama not touched her shoulder to steer her back inside.

Mémère said asking for permission to drink their water spoke well of upbringing. She said many feared these homeless families. Sometimes jewelry, animals, and cash disappeared after households had fed and lodged these people. Some spoke of murder.

46

Later that afternoon, Mama visited them. The father rose from their nest where the children napped under the maple tree. Watching from the kitchen window, Kate hoped Mama wasn't asking them to leave.

Since the auction, Mama had been as ornery as week old stew.

"Hadn't the auction worked out so they could keep the farm now?" Kate asked Tommy. "Wouldn't they be bringing Ben home any day now?" He hadn't answered.

Kate, Leo and Raymond took bread and stew to the Milos family at supper time. The father led his family in grace before they ate under the tree. Mama had told the father they could sleep in the barn for now. He removed his hat to thank her. Mémère sent a needle, thread and snatches of cloth out so the wife could mend her children's threadbare clothes. The oldest boy, Sam, appeared to be around Tommy's age. Edgar, who seemed close to the twins' age, limped badly and stayed close to his mother. The baby was called Teddy. The angel was Alice Jean.

When Kate asked Mama where they came from and why they were here, Mama told her it wasn't polite to ask such things. It wasn't any of their business.

Up close, their squalor was more defined. They smelled like Raymond ten times over. The children's ill-fitting clothes looked as though they might be held together by dirt. Their faces hadn't seen soap for some time.

The blonde mother who appeared young from a distance looked haggard and aged up close. Her watery blue eyes displayed shadowed half moons beneath, her pink dress hung from her frame like a parlor curtain hanging on a vestibule window. She had once been pretty, Kate could tell. Her gaunt face that might have enticed many a beau in years past now barely supported a smile. The baby looked to be less than a year old. Mama made sure they knew to come for milk in the mornings.

Something about the Milos family haunted Kate as she lay in bed that night, twisting her hair. Something she couldn't put her finger on at first. More than how they acted or looked. Or smelled.

Turning from a snorting Mémère, Kate kicked off the sheet, grumbling when her sweaty legs tangled with it. Maybe she should strip off the T-shirt she slept in. Would Mémère awaken from lying next to Kate's wicked state of nakedness? Grab her rosary from the nightstand and slide it through her witch fingers like a serpent slithering through the first apple tree?

That could be her family, Kate realized. Traveling from farm to farm, house to house. Begging for food.

The day after the auction, Kate had mentioned Ben to Mama. She'd been shooed away. A few days later Kate had approached her again and been told in Mama's "don't mention this subject to me again" voice that all was not as it seemed. She would explain everything when the time was right. Meanwhile, Kate must be patient.

So Kate hoed and weeded and watered Ben's garden daily. Sneaked neat piles of corn and lettuce for the deer and bunnies into the woods. She wanted it to be perfect when Ben saw it again. To make him smile.

Mama mumbled to herself in French all the time now.

Mémère was being nice.

Which scared Kate the most.

It almost seemed to Kate as though her family hadn't quite figured out the where or why of their life after the auction. Like they were watching themselves from a distance in a game of checkers.

Awaiting the next move.

What Ben Sees

Unlike most little boys, Ben could sit for the longest time. Outwardly doing nothing. Yet he knew how many times a fly had zipped by him.

Ben watched sun stream through trees and questioned why the sun only shone in the day. Why the moon didn't shine as brightly as the sun. Wondered where shade came from.

As the wind howled on stark autumn days, Ben sang with it. Bowed and swayed with it. Became one with it. Fallen crab apples, soft, sweet, and pungent in their rotting state, blanketed the grass behind the barn like so many forgotten promises.

Mama told Ben to gather the apples and add them to the pigs' slop. Instead Ben collected them and created small piles, the same number of apples in each, for the deer in the woods behind the house.

When ominous black clouds rolled across a spring sky, Ben watched from on high, sitting in the open barn loft door. He wanted to be close to the clouds. Kate told him the god of thunder, Thor, rode the clouds in anger. Ben just sat, absorbing the drama of the impending storm.

He'd stand abruptly, inhale to his toes, smile at Kate, and bid her do the same.

"It smells like the lake looks" he'd announce before settling in for the show.

49

10

For the next several mornings, when Tommy and Kate went to milk Daisy, Nona, and Bony Girl, they found two brimming buckets of warm milk on their milking stools.

A basket of gathered eggs sat in front of the chicken coop and scattered chicken feed covered the ground amidst bawking chickens by 6 a.m.

Kate thought it strange that neither the mother nor father ever came to the door to ask for food. She tried to envision Papa dressed in his three-piece pin striped banker suit, slicked back tawny hair, neatly trimmed mustache, begging at a door. She couldn't.

Tommy said Mr. Milos was too proud to beg. That's why he sent the children to the door if the family needed something.

Until a few days ago.

Kate had watched from the kitchen sink where she washed the breakfast dishes. Hat in hand, Mr. Milos rapped softly at the back door. He'd begged Mama's pardon, shuffled his feet, and smoothed his floppy hat brim as he whispered to her. When he finally made eye contact with Mama, Kate lost her breath, barely saving a plate from the floor.

Tears streamed down the man's face, tracking wet streaks through dirt. He wiped at them with a tattered sleeve, pulling himself upright, raising his trembling chin.

"We'll send Tommy right away," she overheard Mama say.

50

Since there was no money for gas, Mama had Tommy ride Mr. Big to Dykheusen's farm to use their phone.

Dr. Smythe had arrived this morning in his black buggy with Sesame, his high-stepping black horse in harness.

Kate knew without asking why the doctor had been called.

"Jumping a freight train is about as dangerous as driving an automobile full bore off a cliff."

Sam stirred the sputtering orange flames with a long stick. Kate and Tommy swayed backwards, then forward simultaneously, like two boughs in a breeze as sparks exploded from the bonfire.

"You got to stay clear of colored folk and cherry pickers riding the rails," Sam explained. He roughed the fire with his stick. "They aren't the problem, but bulls—railroad cops—and other riders don't much like them." He paused, the firelight casting uneven shadows across his face. "Once…I saw a little Negro boy…about Edgar's age…he tried to jump from a boxcar just as it came to the station and…"

Sitting on logs behind the barn where Papa had burned brush, Kate, Sam, and Tommy talked alone for the first time since the Milos' arrival four days before. Tommy had told Mama they were burning the brush he had culled from the orchard. And they were, but mostly they talked.

Sam gazed into the blue and orange flames without blinking. "He missed."

"Did he get hurt?" Kate asked not really wanting to know.

"Not much when he jumped, but…" Sam straightened before finishing, "…the bulls, they grabbed him and beat him something fierce."

Flame licked logs cracked and popped.

51

"Is...that how your brother hurt his leg? The bulls?" Tommy asked, his voice low and steady.

"Naw. It wasn't the bulls."

They waited.

"I never really talked about it...it wasn't too long ago."

Reading the shiny pain in his eyes through the firelight, Kate said, "You don't have to..."

"Edgar used to flat out run like the wind," Sam surprised them with his announcement. "He used to...where we used to live in Flint...he would win the school picnic race every spring. Even..." Sam's eyes sparkled like fresh rain on leaves "...he'd beat the boys lots older than him. Older than me." His voice rose in glory with his last words.

Kate smiled, nodded, and blinked hard.

"It was at night," Sam continued. "We'd been riding for a couple days in the same boxcar, stopping here and there at a jungle to eat...Mulligan stew or something. Hobos can be good about sharing food. Sometimes. We always stayed together no matter what. Pa said it and meant it. No matter what."

Sam's shoulders slumped forward as he poked the fire. Tommy tossed a section of brush on it, boosting the flames.

"Edgar, he can be a nitwit sometimes." Sam's smile flashed brighter than the fire before dimming. "Pa told us to never go near the bumpers—the couplings between the boxcars—'cause it was dangerous. Everyone knew that. But Edgar...he saw some thin ones on the ground—a dime and a nickel he said—and they were right beneath the..."

Sam nodded fast, his head tilting to one side, his lips pursed.

"He didn't cry or nothin'. He just doesn't talk much anymore and stays close to Mama." He raised his head to address Tommy and Kate directly. "Pa noticed Edgar's leg smelled bad. That's the only reason he asked your Ma to call the doctor."

As the fire dwindled, Kate waited for Tommy to place more brush on it. He didn't.

"What kind of work did your dad do?" Tommy asked. "When you lived in Flint?"

The wide smile that broke out on Sam's face took Kate aback.

"He was an architect." He pronounced the last word in three distinct syllables as if announcing a world champion boxer. His shoulders straightened. "Worked in a big office with a secretary. He went to college."

For the next hour Kate listened as Sam described his family's life riding the rails. He'd seen men pulled under the wheels of a moving train. He spoke of the danger of riding the blinds on the first car behind the engine as you could get in twice as much trouble if caught riding there as stealing a ride in the boxcars. He said if caught riding the tenders attached to the engine, the engineer could drag you off and make you shovel coal for the next hundred miles.

Tommy asked question after question of Sam. About how to catch a freight car, where his family had traveled. How he ate and who to trust.

By the time she and Tommy walked in silence back to the house after quelling the fire with buckets of dirt, Kate had questions too.

Would Edgar's leg ever completely heal?

And why had Tommy asked so many questions of Sam about living a hobo life?

Kate, Fairy Tales, and Peter and Wendy

Kate loved to read to Ben from the fairy tale books and the story of Peter and Wendy that Papa had bought them.

She and Ben would snuggle together at bedtime. Giggling, Ben humming, playing finger games. Mama hated the books Kate loved, claiming their vivid horrors and colorful drawings caused nightmares. She also feared Ben trying to fly like Peter Pan.

Mémère thought they were the Devil's work so she hid them behind Bibles on the bookshelf. Kate thought this strange because if one were to pick up a boring black Bible to read, which she had no intention of doing, there would sit the fat, juicy fairy tales displaying bright blue and red covers, just begging to be read.

Either Mama or Mémère probably figured this out because they finally hid the fairy tale books elsewhere.

But it really didn't matter.

Because Kate just made up different endings to the stories Ben already knew. Better endings.

To her mind, there could never be too many princesses.

And in Kate's version of Little Red Riding Hood, when the wolf ate the grandmother, the old lady was never seen or heard from again.

11

Ben Gone 70 Days
Saturday, August 1, 1931

The Milos family had left that morning after milking the cows and gathering eggs. Mama gave them a flour sack filled with bread, vegetables from the garden, and a container of milk for the baby.

Kate had watched them walk towards the pasture, hand in hand, Edgar limping, Mr. Milos carrying little Teddy.

Sweet angel Alice Jean wearing Ben's overalls.

Mémère, who rarely allowed Kate or her siblings to play without asking forgiveness afterwards, had given Mrs. Milos a pair of Ben's overalls, two pairs of short pants, suspenders, three shirts and his favorite blanket. The yellow blanket he had carried with him everywhere until it had been replaced with the Green Turtle tin.

When Kate expressed her dismay at Ben's clothes being given away, Mama had said Ben had plenty of clothes now; the Milos children didn't.

Kate tried. She bit her tongue every time Mama or Mémère crossed her path. Mama bid her to wash the clothes in the wringer washer, and Kate did. She hung them out, filling three clotheslines that crossed from the black walnut to the sky-scraping maple in the backyard. She fixed Tommy and the twins butter and jam sandwiches which barely passed Raymond's lips before he stole his twin's also, and she had to make more.

Tommy sat in Papa's chair at the dining room table. Kate had accepted that. Papa wasn't coming home.

But when Leo moved to Ben's chair with his second sandwich to stay out of Raymond's reach, Kate didn't try behaving anymore.

"Get off! That's Ben's!"

Gathering Leo's overall straps from the back, she dragged him to his chair, his sandwich clutched in his right hand like it was his last meal.

Tommy continued eating his sandwich, drinking his milk, watching Kate until she disappeared.

Her eyes flashed like stars gone wild, blonde hair strands stuck to her forehead like over-cooked spaghetti as she plowed into the kitchen.

"Ben's never coming home, is he?"

Mama wiped her hands on her daisy embroidered apron with quiet deliberation before facing her daughter.

"Katherine…"

"Why did you give his blanket away? His clothes? When is he coming home?" Her words tumbled out, sharp and loud. She couldn't stop herself from shaking.

"Don't yell at me, young lady," Mama countered. She raised her chin as she spoke. "The Milos family is needier than are we. It's the Christian thing to give…"

"Is it the Christian thing to give your children away?"

Mama faced the stove and continued stirring the black pot. "The auction allowed us to keep the farm for now, but in weeks to come..."

"In weeks to come *what*...?" Kate demanded.

She ignored the fat black fly buzzing by. The blue jays fighting in the maple tree outside the kitchen window.

Instead she noticed gray strands woven throughout Mama's crow-black hair. Circles puffed beneath her dim blue eyes. Her once upon a time hourglass figure swimming in her cotton shift.

How Mama bore a startling resemblance to Mémère.

"After that..." Mama's words evaporated, blending with the steam from the sputtering pot she continued to stir.

Tommy edged the kitchen door open.

"After that..." Mama repeated, her voice low, pregnant with pain, "...after that, Raymond will go to live with my brother Miles in Ontario, and Leo," she sighed, swallowing hard. "Leo will live with my Uncle Pierre in Boston. He may be able to apprentice to him as a carpenter." Mama flashed a fragile smile at Kate and Tommy.

Kate felt as though she was watching all that was unfolding from another place. The way Ben watched storms from the barn loft. This storm had to be happening to someone else. Not her. Not her family.

Where was her shining prince to save her? Where was Papa?

After what seemed like minutes, she heard herself whisper in disbelief, "You're splitting up the twins?"

Their mother nodded fast, stirred harder.

Kate understood now: they were all going to be sent away.

"I want to be with Ben," she blurted. "I don't care where you send me, I just need..."

"Tommy will live with Aunt Bernadette's family in Quebec," their mother continued.

Mouth agape, Tommy stared at his mother. Kate saw this came as a surprise to him. She looked away, unable to suffer his pain-etched expression.

"But I thought..." he said.

"And Kate..." Mama stopped stirring, her eyes absorbed into the pot as if summoning a bubble of hope to its surface, "...will likely go to Ohio to live with my cousin. He lost his wife and needs help with the children." She turned to Kate, her watery blue eyes unfocused. "I've written. I'm awaiting word."

57

The siblings stood statue still.

Leo, followed by Raymond, careened into the kitchen, one towering over the other, punching and yelling. A blue blur of overalls sped out the back porch door as it slammed once hard, twice soft.

Mama inhaled deeply and steadied herself, one hand on the counter, the other holding a dripping wooden spoon. For two seconds she reminded Kate of how she had looked at Papa's funeral.

"Mémère and I will take a room in town at Mrs. Knudson's boarding house. We'll...take in sewing and...make our way." Her voice faltered with the last words. "Ben is well cared for and close by. I had to make sure...that's why when the Samuelsons..."

Kate's growl stumbled up from her gut. "Papa would never have let us split up like this. Papa..."

"...is responsible for what's happening to this family." Their mother's eyes spit blue pain.

"Mama, don't..." Tommy begged, grabbing her arm.

Kate's stare might have burned through her brother's blue checked shirt like it was crisp leaves under Ben's magnifying glass.

"She's old enough to know," Mama snapped at him. "Lord knows, everyone else does."

Kate faced her mother.

Once upon a time...

"Your father made a choice that day," Mama said.

There lived a beautiful princess...

"Mama!" Tommy sounded like a man, his voice strong and full.

Shoulders upright, Kate found her breath. "Papa was killed by the crash when he was crossing the street to buy me my dress!"

The words just spilled out. That's how it had to have happened, she thought. That's why she couldn't find the dress. He'd died on the noble mission of buying her birthday dress.

Mama's head cocked fast, her eyes narrowing with confusion.

"For my birthday!" Kate heard her own high pitched plea. "He was killed...on his way to buy me my..."

Mama placed her hands on Kate's shoulders, her words tender and hoarse.

"Your father was killed by a crash, but...it wasn't..."

Kate smelled mint from the herb garden outside the kitchen window.

"He lost the farm in the stock market crash," Mama continued, garnering strength with the truth. "Then he used bank monies to buy more stock. When it was discovered..."

Tommy slumped onto a chair, cradling his forehead in both hands, rocking. Kate didn't recognize him. Where had her family gone?

"He was crossing the street to buy me my dress when the accident..." Kate's voice crumbled, wandered into a distant place.

"It was no accident. He stepped in front..."

Kate backed away, pushing Tommy's words away with open palms. The ice box handle stabbed her in the back.

Dashing one of Mama's precious tea cups to the floor, Kate staggered out the back door.

To the only place she could go.

The Cemetery

Kate had never been one to pray. Except at bedtime when Mama made her and in church with Mémère's beady eyes boring into the back of Kate's head like a woodpecker drilling tree bark for bugs.

Since Papa had been killed by the crash, Kate had not prayed one bit.

Kate asked Ben if he would like to visit Papa's grave, wondering if he understood any of what had happened. He said he'd like to see Papa again which worried Kate. Did he expect to see Papa alive? She explained several times about the accident and Papa being dead. Ben seemed thoughtful after she spoke but confirmed that he would like to visit the cemetery.

Kate wanted to ride Tommy's bicycle, but the roads were too hilly to carry Ben in the front wire basket. She wouldn't have anything to do with riding a horse, so they walked the three miles to the cemetery which, Mémère had declared more than once, had accepted Papa to her great relief.

A light spring rain misted over them that late April morning. Sometimes Kate lugged Ben on her back for a ways. He hummed and picked wildflowers along the winding dirt road, his Green Turtle Cigar tin swinging, squeaking at his side.

Kate watched him closely. He sang a ditty as he placed a drawing of himself and Kate on Papa's unadorned grave.

"Do you understand that Papa is gone?" she finally asked in a cemetery voice. Tilting his head, smiling small, Ben arranged a loose bouquet of purple, white and gold wildflowers below the drawing.

"Papa's not gone," Ben lisped, one hand entwining with his sister's. "Papa asked me to keep singing to him even if I couldn't see him no more. I promised."

He showed Papa his Green Turtle Cigar tin, blew a kiss at the grave, and waved good-bye as they turned to leave.

12

That Evening

Cardinal "chip chip" vied with the singsong whippoor-will to create an uneven evening song.

Doughy gray clouds broke to reveal a whimsical gold that infused the lake; purples, oranges, and pinks trickled into the gold lake like spilled pots of paint.

Only at this time of day. Because that's when the ogre had been killed by the handsome prince.

Allowing the boat to drift, Kate kept one oar in the water for steering.

She'd never come here alone before. Never without Ben. Yet today she'd been here since running out of the kitchen at lunch. Nobody had come for her. She was glad.

She promised herself the next time she came to the lake it would be with Ben, and she would let him row. All by himself.

How long ago had it been since she'd gone to the school social instead of to the lake with Ben? Languished over stupid Harvey Vandervelde who couldn't find a flask of gin if it was stuck in his eye? Weeks? Years? Time had lost all meaning. She hadn't seen Margaret or any of her friends for so long.

Mosquitoes stung, and she swatted, squashing one on her shoulder, another above her boot. *Why bother,* she thought. *Why not just let them eat me alive here and now?*

It had been a lifetime since Papa had died. Forever since Ben had been gone.

If only she'd known that night would have been her last time at the lake with Ben. If only she could take it back.

Did they make Ben eat meat at the Samuelson's? Could he draw? She was sure he couldn't say good night to a lake every evening.

Could he tend his own garden? Dance in it? What was he doing right now? Was he thinking of her? Crying for her?

Both oars wiggled in their locks as Kate bent forward, folding herself into her arms. Closing her eyes, she watched Ben dance, pajamas and hair flying. Heard his garden song, high pitched and joyful.

Kate sighed, leaning to let a finger trail in the water. Why didn't the ripples make sounds?

Only lavender blushed through the treetops now, night blue moments away.

Thick cricket noise see-sawed through the air. It did smell like just before a storm here.

A dragonfly landed on the boat's edge, flitting in all its opalescent beauty, before disappearing into twilight.

Like Tinker Bell, thought Kate.

If only Papa were alive, they would all be together. Stay together.

But Papa wasn't coming home. Tommy had been enthralled with Sam Milos' tales of the hobo life. Was Tommy thinking about leaving? Especially now that he knew Mama was planning on sending him away, too?

She ignored the tightening in her chest, the shaking of her hands.

This couldn't be real; this couldn't be happening. All of them. To different places.

Hands clasped to keep them from shaking, Kate closed her eyes. Papa couldn't come home. But if she brought Ben home, all would be well. She didn't know the why or how of it, she just knew it. Believed it.

Like Tinker Bell.

One clap startled the night. Another.

Clap if you believe in fairies and Tinker Bell will live...

"I believe." Her whisper and hand clap were lost amidst the constant of evening bird chatter.

"I believe in Ben..." sounded louder. Two claps became three, three became more, and her plea echoed louder and louder between harder claps as dusk disappeared into dark. Flocks of sparrows soared as one into the edge of night.

"I believe in Ben...I believe in Ben...I believe in Ben...I believe in Ben...I believe in Ben...I believe in Ben...I believe in Ben...I believe in Ben...I believe in Ben..."

Kate's voice soared, hoarse yet strong, her hands steady as they clapped in even cadence.

Imploring the night to believe in the magic of Ben.

Sailboats and Castles

"One day we'll sail away in a big beautiful sailboat and live in a castle," Kate promised, lifting an oar. *"There'll be servants to do our every bidding."*

"A sailor boat?" Ben asked.

"No, a sailboat," Kate corrected. *"A boat with big high sheets that the wind blows to make it move."*

Ben watched a school of minnows jerk and slow beneath a mote-laden sun shard.

"Will Mama and Tommy be there?"

Kate rowed harder, her short, blonde hair bobbing with each pull. She paused to wave a cloud of gnats from her face.

"No," Kate huffed through a row. She saw his eyes that suited one so serious, but not so young. *"Maybe Tommy."*

Ben skimmed the water with three fingers. He counted the ripples in the darkening shine of lake. Noted their equal distance from one another. Wondered why they didn't make a sound.

"I want to row."

"You don't row a sailboat, silly."

"I want to row now," he whispered.

Kate sighed. *"Maybe next time. It's getting dark."*

Oars dipped, dripped, and dipped, counterpointing a female cardinal call and cricket purr. A dwindling tangerine sun crowned treetops encircling the lake.

"Can I sing my song on the sailor boat?" he asked with triple lisp.

"If you want."

Gnat clouds escorted the rowboat to shore. A column of sun shimmered gold across the water.

"Will we still say good night to the lake?" asked Ben.

A fish broke the surface in silence several feet away.

"Yes, Ben Boy."

13

Ben Gone 79 Days
Monday, August 10, 1931

She saw him.

The upright, silvery blue woman held his hand as they walked along across the street from Kate.

He didn't skip or run. Or zig zag in his silly walk. He plodded in what looked to be new Buster Brown shoes that fit.

His clothes looked crisp in the August heat. The Green Turtle Cigar tin swung from his right hand. His hair had been cut; the blond patch survived.

Ben.

Shoving people on the sidewalk without apology, Kate worked her way to where she could see him better. Where he could see her.

Trucks and automobiles jiggled by one another on the street, honking; people herded through the crosswalk in front of Van Ark's pharmacy toward the Farmer's Market. Through a kaleidoscope of colorful clothing, dark automobiles, and trucks, from beneath the red and white striped awning announcing Betsy's Dress and Millinery, Kate called to him.

He started to turn towards her, from the shadows toward the sun, the blond patch more pronounced. Mrs. Samuelson must have felt him pull her hand because she gently jerked him forward.

"I'm Ben's sister!" Kate yelled, her voice high and hard like the trill of a bird in distress.

They continued to walk, Ben shuffling, Kate barely breathing.

"I'm his sister!" she yelled louder, pushing forward, several passersby frowning at her.

Without missing a step, upright Mrs. Samuelson, in her silvery blue dress with a matching feathered hat declared in a voice that Kate thought must sound like Cinderella's stepmother—a voice that Kate would remember all of her life:

"He doesn't have a sister anymore."

Ben disappeared without ever looking at her.

But before he was rushed around the corner, she saw them.

Five sweet Ben fingers wiggling—beckoning—her from the handle of his little tin box.

Snatches of conversations, dogs barking, children crying, a man sweeping, horns honking—a blur of harsh noises and whirling colors sucked Kate into a cloud. For seconds she forgot who she was or why she stood there.

Watching Ben walk away from her.

The silvery blue woman's words echoing.

He doesn't have a sister anymore.

Kate felt Papa's presence. Had he stood as she now stood? A black Model T pick-up truck barreled towards her. Gloom gobbled her up with stark hunger. She peered directly into the eyes of the driver.

Like Papa?

As if in a dream she heard her name called. The driver's eyes were blue. She could move. She didn't.

Brakes screamed, people screamed, and Kate found herself lying on the sidewalk with Tommy on top of her.

"Mother of…what were you doing!" Tommy screamed, although he needn't have, lying two inches from her. She didn't flinch. She wasn't truly aware yet.

It was a whisper. "Ben."

Sitting up, Tommy brushed off his stained knees and calmed a lady in beige who wanted to call the police. The truck idled in the middle of the street, bushels of sweetcorn scattered from its bed across the pavement and sidewalk like so much Rumpelstiltskin straw.

"Jumpin…are you all right, little lady?"

Kneeling on one leg, the driver wore dingy overalls and held his wide straw farmer's hat in his hand, rubbing the brim back and forth between his fingers like a child's favorite sleep toy.

Kate sat up and nodded. Sitting on the curb, Tommy had stuffed his head between his knees, puffing for air. He stared at his sister with utter bewilderment.

"Why didn't you move when I called?"

With the crack in his voice, Kate thought he almost sounded twelve again.

"I saw Ben."

Tommy stood, unbending slowly. "You okay?"

She didn't answer. She still seemed to be sharing space with Papa in the street.

The black pick-up truck barreling down on her.

Inviting.

The crowd had dissipated, people going about their business. Adults shaking their heads at the recklessness of youth.

Kate knew it wasn't recklessness.

And it didn't touch only youth.

He doesn't have a sister anymore.

Ben's Invisible Friend

His name was Prince Alfred the Great.

He arrived shortly after Papa was killed by the crash.

Bejeweled and handsome, Prince Alfred the Great shared everything with Ben. He ate, slept, and played with Ben. With Papa gone, there was an empty chair at the dining room table. Ben insisted Prince Alfred sit at the table to share their meals. The Prince spoke a language that only Ben could understand. Or hear.

The good Prince did not eat meat although he had a hearty appetite for hot buttered cornbread. Ben fixed his plate for him.

Ben whispered to the Prince and held his hand so he would not become lost in this foreign land of common people. Tommy kindly allowed the Prince to sleep on their bedroom floor as long as his Royal Highness did not snore.

Prince Alfred the Great and Ben seemed to share many a secret.

The Prince never appeared when Ben was with Kate.

14

That Evening

Kate hadn't eaten much at supper that evening. Neither Mama nor Mémère had mentioned the afternoon's events. She knew they knew.

Had someone yelled for Papa to look out when he crossed the street that day?

Had he heard them?

Heeded them?

Moonlight streamed through the open bedroom window later that night, creating lacy curtain patterns on the far wall. Mémère snored beside her. Crickets clicked, and frogs ponged in the distance. Everything looked and sounded and smelled normal.

But it wasn't normal.

He doesn't have a sister anymore.

Every time she closed her eyes, she relived the black truck careening towards her. Witnessed the red plaid shirt, straw hat, the gaping mouthed horror of the blue-eyed driver.

Kate knew she must have slept because she dreamed.

Papa stood across the street, yelling for her to look out for the truck. She dreamed of Ben running towards her in his awkward gait, arms outstretched. Just as he reached her, fingers wiggling for her, she woke with a start, breath rasping, her cotton nightie sweat soaked, arms reaching for Ben.

Had Papa felt the same emptiness on that February day as she had felt today?

Moist white nightie clinging to her, she padded barefoot to the window. Not a curtain stirred. The outline of Ben's garden below emerged as she gazed.

Sunflowers, now twice as tall as Ben, reached toward the starry skies as he had reached for her in her dreams.

Within minutes she was knotting her nightie above her knees, smacking Ben's garden with a hoe. The moon illuminated waist-high corn stalks, lettuce and beans, all green and prospering because of Kate.

She picked stones from the garden, building a small pile along the edge in case Ben wanted them. Ben liked stones. Crumbling dirt scratched at her bare feet as she stepped from row to row, breaking up the rain-deprived soil. After weeding, she lugged two green watering cans from the windmill well and sprinkled the garden evenly the way Ben liked. Row by row. She filled them again.

With every strike of the hoe, drop of water, every pluck of an unwanted weed, Kate's heartache diminished.

She sighed, her breathing calmed at last. The night felt so still.

Like a heart had stopped beating.

Ben's scarecrow appeared forlorn despite its smiley face, its straw hat askew. Kate heard a rabbit nibbling lettuce. As her eyes adjusted to her surroundings, she found its profile, watched its whiskers twitch, ears flutter. She hoed with a softer touch now, hoping not to scare the rabbit. Ben would want it to stay. The "chunk chunk" of the hoe chanted. A "moon song," she knew Ben would call it.

She hummed as she knew Ben would hum. Danced a little dance as Ben would.

The night sky mutated to violet and melon along treetops. The stars twinkled less.

A new day blossomed.

Kate smelled the earth, the peas, and corn. Listened to sporadic sparrow chatter, throaty mourning dove coos. This was Ben's garden.

This was Ben.

Her right hand clasped and unclasped in anticipation of clasping his wiggling fingers.

A grace shimmered within her like heat lightning before a storm.

Upstairs she stripped off her soiled nightgown and climbed into bed, pulling the sheet over her. Mémère snorted.

Kate's hands folded across her stomach as prim as a preacher's wife at tea.

Fresh sun spilled buttercup yellow across her pillow.

Everything would be fine. She would be with Ben again.

Because Ben still had a sister.

Dancing at Dawn in Ben's Garden

The dingy drop seat to Ben's long underwear bagged and flapped around him as he danced in the early morning moonlight.

The twins had promised him that if he danced in the garden at dawn, his beans and corn would grow faster.

Ben's arms flailed to a secret rhythm, his eyes rolling back into his head. He swayed and swirled like a weather vane in a storm. His hair ruffled, his small body almost lost amidst the movement and flutter of cloth.

Kate thought he looked like he belonged in the Baptist revival meetings in the big white tents they passed on the drive to Mass. Kate always said out loud how much fun that looked like. It didn't seem to create the heart palpitations in Mémère she'd hoped for. But it did put Mémère to prayer, her long bony fingers skittering her rosary beads like one of Ben's favorite water bugs skittering over the water.

Ben would awaken Kate with a soft tickle and giggle, careful not to wake Mémère snoring beside her. Kate had warned him the twins were just teasing about the garden.

But Ben took his garden seriously. And Kate took Ben seriously.

So together they danced barefoot to morning birdsong. Holding hands, Ben's skivvies flapping, Kate's nightgown flouncing.

Until Mémère scolded them and made them wash their feet before breakfast.

15

Hoboes, railroad bulls, mangy curs, and children, wandered, yelled, barked, and cried throughout the freight yard.

This was not a nightmare, Kate had to remind herself more than once.

Steaming tin coffee pots offered a greasy brown liquid that looked and smelled like fresh mud. That combined with the sight of hoboes throwing wilted lettuce, onions, ears of corn, dandelions, and Bill Durham tobacco into black kettles of what Sam had referred to as Mulligan stew snatched her back into reality.

Kate noticed several families huddled together and wondered about the Milos family.

Adjusting the flour sack thrown over her shoulder, she checked her pants pockets—$1.12.

All the money she had left from selling empty medicine bottles to Mr. Van Ark. Inside the flour sack she'd placed two cornbread squares, several slices of bread, a few personal items, and a flat fifty tin of Lucky Strike cigarettes. The latter she'd stolen from Carlstrom's Mercantile yesterday right after Timothy the box boy had told her about the Samuelsons moving.

She'd gone into Carlstrom's Mercantile with Mama's short grocery list after she and Tommy had sold the eggs and cream. Since he couldn't buy any, Tommy was reading detective magazines a few stores down at the pharmacy.

Mémère's gold pocket watch could be heard ticking loud-ly whenever they went into town.

Timothy was closer to Tommy's age than to hers. She en-vied him his box boy job but had never liked him. He teased the younger children at school. He also constantly picked his nose, wiping its contents on his shirt front. Kate cringed at the memory of Margaret saying he liked her. Never would she have spoken to him had he not spoken first.

"So, you hear probably no school come September?" he piped while throwing Kate's small bag of cornmeal into the box. His voice squeaked like that of a frightened mouse. "School Board said can't pay no teacher."

Kate nodded, moving a few feet away. It didn't matter to her. Neither she nor her brothers would likely be living here by September anyway.

She signed the credit chit without Mama's flare and lifted the light box, planning on meeting Tommy. He owed her for making her buy groceries alone. After three steps her feet stopped. Her gut lunged as though being torn apart by forty plow horses. She swallowed the lump in her throat. Was it weeks or days now? When would she be without Tommy?

"I read about your brother."

Kate froze before turning to face the squeaky, skinny nose picker.

"Which brother?" she whispered, the cardboard box low-ering in her arms with the weight of his words.

That's how she discovered Samuelsons had moved to Traverse City four days earlier. Mr. Samuelson had bought a car dealership there with his brother. Timothy had read it in the paper. Thought Ben had it made living with such a high and mighty family. He was just starting to ask if Kate and the rest of her siblings might be lucky enough to join Ben when she lurched out the door.

She hadn't even felt like crying. Not one bit. It was like the morning, weeks after Papa had died—after the accident—

when she had awoken and not cried for the first time. Like a switch had flicked inside her.

It was time to stop worrying about what had been and started thinking about what to do next.

Better to run away with Ben than be sent away alone.

Scampering to the pharmacy, she shoved the grocery box at Tommy with his magazine still in his hand and ran back to the mercantile. As Kate sidled out the door with Mrs. Rossevelt and her four children, offering to hold the hand of little Arthur as she managed her groceries...Timothy watched her closely.

If he noticed the outline of a tin of Lucky Strikes pressed to her hip under her skirt, he hadn't said anything. She forgave him his nose and voice.

She'd thought about asking Tommy to come with her but decided he probably wouldn't go with her, and he'd feel obliged to tell Mama. It wasn't fair to put him in that position. Just because she had become a liar and thief didn't mean Tommy had to become one.

Here she stood, alone in a freight yard as night approached, having stolen clothes, food, and cigarettes, trying to remember all that Sam had told them about riding the rails that night by the fire.

Children and women should not travel alone.

Just about any man or boy could be bribed with cigarettes.

Don't talk to people unless absolutely necessary.

Eat and drink whenever you can, no matter what it is.

Always sleep with your back against the wall.

Don't trust anyone, even adult hoboes.

Never jump onto a moving boxcar.

And, most importantly, stay clear of the bulls.

Ben's Numbers and Words

Kate tried. *Again and again. But the letters just wouldn't stick.*

She wrote them on her small chalkboard slate for Ben to read. He repeated each the first time she told him. But he couldn't tell what it was the next time he saw it. And rarely thereafter.

Kate didn't recall learning to read. She just knew she had always been able to. Before going to school. Before the twins could.

But letters and words and Ben didn't mix.

Yet he could glance at a basket of eggs and say exactly how many were in it every time. Knew how many green beans it took to fill a quart jar when helping Mama and Mémère with the canning. If Kate said, "14 plus 35 take away 12 plus 55 take away 24" he could tell her "68" before Mémère could say "If wishes were horses, then beggars would ride."

Numbers stuck to Ben just fine.

16

The freight yard quieted as darkness fell.

At least it seemed to Kate there was less fighting.

Yet every smell, sound, and sensation was strange to her. She'd found a spot to sleep. Just dropped her sack onto the dirt and laid down.

Curled into a ball, head resting on her flour sack, silk purse tucked between her knees and stomach, Kate didn't sleep. She struggled to find a section of hair beneath her cap, but it was too slick to twist.

No wonder Sam had referred to this place as a jungle.

Several musty stained mattresses hosted sleeping hoboes across the yard which bordered the train station. Hoboes of every size, gender, and age sat on crates and boxes around snippets of fire that added heat and smoke to the already thick summer night.

Hitching a ride to Grand Rapids dressed as a boy had been scary yet eye-opening. It was surprising how kind people could be. It had taken her two rides to get to the Grand Rapids freight yard: a short ride in a wagon and a much longer one in a truck with windows stuck up so it was impossible to breathe.

Wearing Tommy's shirt and Leo's pants and a newsboy cap pulled low over her blonde brow, she'd slicked her chin-length hair behind her ears with Papa's *Murray's Superior Hair Dressing Pomade*. It still sat on the shelf in the bathroom next to Mama's lilac talc tin. At first Kate wasn't go-

79

ing to take the tin of pomade with her. But Kate figured she might need to look like a boy for some time in her travels with Ben.

Plus the pomade smelled like Papa.

Kate was sure she had walked at least a mile before the first automobile passed. She only hailed those that had ladies or girls in them to feel safer. Once she'd been forced to stoop and pretend to tie her boot when Mr. Timmons clanked by in his Model T truck, belching a smoke trail into the twilight. Kate couldn't help but recall the lemon cake Mrs. Timmons had brought that day that seemed so very long ago. Her taste buds twanged with the memory of its yellow tartness.

She'd told Mama she was going to the lake for awhile after dinner and chores. Sitting in the parlor mending as she did every evening, Mama had smiled and told her to be home by dark. The image of Mama's hand sewing in an exact rhythm over and under, over and under, resonated through Kate like a favorite song.

She wouldn't be home by dark. Or by light.

Having hidden her flour sack, clothes, and purse by the lake earlier, all she had to do was change into Leo and Tommy's stolen clothes and be off to Grand Rapids.

She tried to say good night to the lake, but her voice failed her on three tries.

An older lady whose brown man's fedora topped her stringy gray hair hobbled toward where Kate lay in the freight yard. Kate's stomach scrunched and unscrunched; should she pretend to be sleeping?

"Little boy," the lady said, her voice lighter and smoother than Kate would have imagined.

The lady offered a tin cup. Remembering Sam's words, Kate drank whatever it was, struggling to keep it in her stomach. Something stuck in her teeth but she didn't want to know what it was. When she smiled her thanks, the woman stiffened.

80

"You alone, Missy?" the fedora lady asked, scanning the area.

Taken aback at being called "Missy," Kate answered in a low guttural voice, Leo's cap pulled down. "Uh, no...I...my mother and father are out with my brothers," Kate stuttered. "They'll be right back."

The woman's skirts spread on the ground like a small flood as she squatted to meet Kate's eyes. She shoved the fedora up so her round face and squinty eyes opened to the night. A flickering fire showcased craggy wrinkles. Kate wondered if she was the same age as Mémère.

"Don't be talking to strangers, Missy." The woman shook her finger at Kate, emphasizing the last word. "Those dimples of yours will give you away every time."

The woman stood.

"You taking the sleeping cars or morning run?" she asked.

Kate decided at this point she had no choice but to trust the woman.

"I want to get to Traverse City. I...I'm not sure which train to get...to take."

The fedora woman glanced at the hoboes sitting and sleeping around the dwindling fire.

"Same as us." She pointed into the distance. Kate struggled to follow her direction. "Pullman cars stop there. Sleeper resort train to Traverse." She nodded more to herself than to Kate. "Stay close. We'll be leavin' soon enough."

The woman grinned, her lack of top teeth evident even in the dark.

"We're goin' first class all the way. Might just get myself a haircut on the train." Plucking off her fedora, she smoothed her grey rat-tail hair. "Maybe take a tub bath and get myself a big bouquet of red roses just like the swells."

The woman's husky laugh mutated into a moist, hacking cough without end as she returned to her group, spat into the fire with a splattering hiss, and settled in. Hunched and somber, they reminded Kate of vultures awaiting first dibs on a fresh carcass.

She curled harder, as though she might curl herself into another place if she curled hard enough.

My mother and father are out with my brothers...

Never would she see Papa again.

What of Mama and Mémère? Leo and Raymond?

The woman knew Kate was a girl. Traveling alone. Maybe she should have asked Tommy to come with her.

Once upon a time...

Nothing.

Once upon a time there was a...

Emptiness. No princes or princesses. No sparkling dresses of Lucerne or any other shade of blue. No magical fairy dust or flying away to Neverland.

No happily ever after.

No matter how many times Kate tried to conjure a fairy tale from her extensive repertoire, as she did in times like this, all that came to her were the sounds of coughing, crying, and raucous laughter. The stench of urine and unbathed bodies in the August heat.

Kate had lost her fairy tales.

When she found Ben, everything would be fine. Somehow.

"Missy, best get your belongings and come with us," yelled the fedora woman.

"Train's comin'."

82

Radio

On Sunday evenings, after Ben had been properly tucked into his side of the bed that he shared with Tommy, he pretended to read while awaiting Kate's return.

At 9:30 she came. Pretending to check on him. Drowning in Leo's old drop-bottom pajamas, Ben would creep downstairs hand in hand with Kate to sit on the bottom step around the corner from the parlor. Mama and Mémère couldn't see them from where they sat tatting and darning socks. But Tommy and Papa could. Papa was the one who turned the static-ridden boxy brown Philco radio up so Ben and Kate could hear it.

Ben's huge blue eyes would become huger, bluer. His shoulders would scrunch and long fingers rub together in delightful anticipation of hearing the low, evil male voice.

"What evil lurks in the hearts of man... yuh, uh, uh. The Shadow knows."

When he heard the man's cackling laugh, Ben had to cover his mouth tightly with both hands so Mama and Mémère wouldn't hear his fearful glee. Halfway through the show, Ben would yawn, and Kate would carry him back to bed, his legs wrapped about her waist, his head bobbing on her shoulder.

17

Kate followed the fedora lady.

Several in her group watched for the bulls while others threw duffle bags and sacks into the boxcar, climbed aboard and helped lift the others in.

Remembering Sam's warning about trusting hoboes, Kate hadn't wanted to throw her sack up. She'd stuffed her purple silk purse inside it for safekeeping and most boys didn't carry purple silk purses. Someone yanked her sack from her and tossed it into the stink of the boxcar. She remembered the shadow of a man's hand beckoning her. She'd hesitated, unsure of this world she was entering.

But her sack was on board so she had to go. A man grabbed her arm and reeled her in, her cap almost falling off with the act. When everyone was inside, they slid the doors closed.

"Not a word," someone whispered.

What small coolness the night air had offered remained outside the boxcar.

The boxcar creaked, groaned and shivered as it started to move. Pine tar and creosote smells mingled with body and tobacco odors. The jerking motions of the car whipped everyone uniformly to one side, then the other.

When Kate's eyes grew accustomed to the interior, she realized many others had been in the boxcar when her group arrived.

Including the Milos family.

❖　❖　❖

Pulling her cap down almost to her nose, Kate watched from beneath its bill.

Two groups of teenage boys filled one corner. They lounged about with straw in their mouths. One boy played the harmonica until a man told him to stop. Families and the fedora lady's group sat and stretched out close to the walls.

Seeing Mr. Milos, Sam, Edgar and the others tore at Kate. They reminded her of home. Of Tommy.

But she couldn't let them know she was there. Mr. Milos would surely send her home.

Head down, Kate shuffled her way to the teen boys in the corner, sitting next to the dark haired harmonica player. Snapping her cap over her eyes, she pretended to sleep against her sack.

Back to the wall.

She figured in this corner she was more likely to be taken for a boy anyway. Something bit her and she scratched at it. She briefly wondered what time it was before the jostling of the train and lack of air invited sleep.

Her dream was of a much younger Tommy riding his bicycle up and down their drive, Papa cheering him on. Tommy wore a striped shirt while Papa wore overalls. Mama watched from the porch smiling and waving.

"Got a smoke, kid?"

After a few pokes in the ribs, Kate realized the dark haired teenager was talking to her. She had no idea where she was when she awoke. Sudden realization made her long for her dream.

"Nah," Kate growled.

"Lemme see."

Before she could lift her head, her flour sack disappeared from beneath it. She tried to grab it back, but noticed others were watching her corner and decided to let him have the cigarettes. That's what she'd brought them for anyway. To bribe and make peace.

The smile spreading across the teen's stubbled face took Kate by surprise. Maybe he hadn't expected to find so many cigarettes. He could have them all.

"What's your name, kid?"

She hadn't thought about that.

"Tommy," she answered.

He'd removed the tin of Lucky Strikes and passed the cigarettes around to his friends, keeping the tin for himself.

Leaning close enough so Kate could smell his fetid breath and feel the stubble on his chin, he whispered, "Sure it ain't Thomasina?"

Tree Climbing Ben

"Ben Boy, that's high enough," Kate called.

As she motioned for him to come down, his slight frame disappeared amidst the boughs many feet up the maple tree. A breeze blew, making Kate hold her breath.

"I can seeeee faaaarrrr," he sang.

She waited. She knew he would stay up there all day if he had his way. With the birds and squirrels. She'd told him once he was part squirrel. He'd become excited, thinking he would sprout a busy tail, and cried when she'd told him otherwise.

"Ben, what do you see?"

"I see...smokes from chimneys and...church tops and...a truck coming down the road."

"That's enough, Ben."

"I'm a bird!"

Remembering how Ben had once broken an arm jumping from the barn loft in an attempt to fly, Kate told him he might row the boat that night if he came down now.

87

18

She couldn't run anymore.

It hurt to breathe. Her right arm hung useless at her side, her ribs throbbed with every step, and she tasted blood from her eyebrow.

Maybe her nose. It didn't matter.

Kate decided the dark-haired teen must have figured out she was a girl when he saw the purple silk purse in her sack. Maybe when she spoke. She knew she'd never smiled at him. He'd teased her about being a girl in private on the train. She longed to sit with the Milos family. But she couldn't.

Not if she wanted to find Ben.

The teen had finally given her back her sack after eating the food. She'd forced herself to stay awake the rest of the trip by weeding and hoeing and watering Ben's garden in her mind. Vegetable by vegetable. Row by row.

Would Ben ever see his garden again?

Once the train pulled into the Traverse City station, Kate had jumped off as fast as she could amidst the scattering of hoboes and ran.

It seemed to be noon or close to it. Sweaty, thirsty, stomach rumbling, she lumbered towards town where she figured car dealerships might be. The thought of a crisp cold Orange Crush made her throat ache. She didn't have enough spit to whistle or call chickens to feed.

That's when she smelled it. Cigarettes and vanilla.

Heard their laughing.

The harmonica.

Kate walked faster, but their legs were longer.

Hoping to find a group of people to blend into, she glanced about the neighborhood of shacks and shanties and noticed only an old man sleeping in the shade.

The Milos family was nowhere to be seen.

Tired, hungry, and feeling like she had been away from home forever, Kate ran.

They'd pulled her into heavy bushes by the tracks. A crack resonated, she both felt and heard it, when her right arm was wrenched behind her back and twisted. One grabbed Leo's cap and stuffed it on his head, preening and laughing.

She fought. She fought like she fought Leo and Raymond, kicking and screaming and spitting and biting. It was when she bit the biggest one with the blond hair that he'd walloped her across the face with his fist. Stunned, she lost focus and found herself flat on the ground, the short thick teen kneeling on her ribs.

"Well, little Miss Thomasina's got some fire in her, don't she?" the harmonica player singsonged.

She slapped and pushed with her left arm, the right limp in an abyss of agony.

When a man yelled at them to stop, for a split second they hesitated. She kicked the harmonica player hard in his groin, bit the hand on her shoulder with all her might, and darted through them without looking back.

She ran and ran until she had no breath, and then she ran some more.

Finally, when her legs refused to move, she plopped onto some grass and lay still as night.

Mémère's Alarm Clock

Ben wasn't punished when he spread all the working parts of Mémère's Big Ben Westclock alarm clock across the back porch floor one spring afternoon.

When Ben was four and a half, Kate informed him the alarm clock by the side of Mémère's bed bore his name.

That's when he had decided it should be his.

Mémère searched and easily found the missing timepiece in Ben and Tommy's room. She placed it back next to her bed, instructing Ben to leave it there.

But Ben wasn't done with it; he hadn't yet figured out how it worked.

That's when he had borrowed his namesake shiny brass clock with large, black numbers again and taken it apart. Every cog, wheel, spring, coil, and gear of its guts lay spread across the porch floor in groupings according to size and what Ben determined to be their function.

When Mémère instructed him to put it back together as best he could, Ben did.

The alarm clock worked fine.

19

Kate lay in a blanket of green grass the likes of which she had never known.

Sinking her fingers into the mesh of blades, she watched clouds meander in a silvery blue sky. She felt like she could stay there forever. Sleep forever.

Midday sun seared her eyes. She ignored the riveting ache in her arm and side.

She no longer tasted fresh blood.

Rich people lived in these neighborhoods. Every house was a mansion with red and pink potted geraniums by the driveways and along the front walkways. Flower gardens looked like how a million songs might sound.

Lush lawns, green and thick, looked the way she'd always imagined God's front yard might look if He had one.

She glanced around a manicured hedge. Her body and soul sighed.

Only prim nannies pushing fancy baby buggies and well dressed folks walking little dogs with bows traveled through this neighborhood.

No hobo teenagers.

Willing herself to stand, Kate noticed a maid not much older than herself hanging laundry in a beautiful side yard three houses down. A white fence surrounded the shady yard that was bordered by perfect, rubbery looking hedges. The red-headed girl wore a crisp blue cotton dress with a blindingly white apron and maid's cap.

Kate wondered if she might get such a job. She'd planned on taking Ben with her on the trains, but now she realized that couldn't happen.

Standing at the fence, Kate watched her hang laundry until the maid gave a small shriek and covered her mouth. The maid dropped the green blouse in her hand into a wicker basket and moved toward Kate as though she were a wounded dog.

"Are you...are you needing a doctor, Miss?"

Kate thought the maid's lilt spoke of an Irish accent. It sounded like Mrs. Finnegan, who used to play the organ at church.

"No, I...I'm fine. I just..."

"Can I get you a glass of water? It's hot enough to boil spit on the sidewalk."

"That would be...thank you."

Kate didn't want to sit down, afraid she would be unable to get back up.

A nanny clad in a striped blouse and navy blue skirt pushing a baby carriage covered with netting snarled at Kate with her eyes as she passed by without slowing down.

Kate realized how out of place she must look here. She shoveled her left hand through her slick hair. Leo's cap had never made it back to her head.

The maid returned with a glass of water and what looked to be a sandwich wrapped in butcher paper. And a cool wet cloth.

"Here you are," she said, handing the glass to Kate who swallowed it in almost three desperate gulps. She handed her the cloth which Kate immediately used to wipe her bloody face. The maid whispered, "And here's a little something to tide you over," as she passed the wrapped sandwich through a top fence rail.

Kate's stomach blasted when it knew food was near, but she planned on saving it in case she and Ben needed it.

"Thank you so much. I don't want to get you in trouble..."

"Bridget. Me name's Bridget. No, the missus is at club, and it's just me and the rest of the servants this afternoon." She looked Kate over. "You might need to see a doctor, if you don't mind me saying so, Miss."

"I'm fine. Thank you," Kate lied.

Starting to hand the bloody cloth back to the maid, the maid raised her hand to let Kate know she could keep it.

"Do you know a family named Samuelson?" Kate asked.

The maid tilted her round freckled face. "No, I don't believe so."

"They probably just moved in a few days ago."

Bridget shook her head.

Bidding Bridget good day, Kate walked past the eye-popping mansions, holding onto the white picket fence for support.

Her ears buzzed, but she ignored it.

Block after block, people steered away from her. They passed her by as though she were a rowboat daring to enter their elegant harbor.

Kate knew inside she was a sailboat. She'd promised Ben once. A hundred years ago. They'd sail away on a sailboat. With a big white sail. She and Ben. Maybe Tommy. Yes, Tommy. She could almost feel the water now. Cool. If she closed her eyes...

She didn't know why she stopped. Appraising her surroundings, she saw she stood in front of a house.

If she closed her eyes she could feel the water...

Opening her eyes, the mansion to her right dripped with red, pink, purple, and yellow flowers along the walkway, the

93

driveway, hanging from the porch. A bronze mansion with not one, but two golden turrets, the likes of which she'd only seen in fairy tale books.

Like the castle she'd promised Ben they would live in someday.

Pink and white flowering trees graced the green lawn that was the size of Van Ark's pharmacy.

She scanned the side yard. She smelled roses. A new flat seated swing with a rod in front half swung from a maple tree.

Her throbbing head now matched her throbbing arm and ribs. The buzzing in her ears sounded like thousands of Big Ben alarm clocks. A reddish haze of pain swamped her vision.

Yet she saw this clearly.

Beneath the swing, nestled within the bubbling veins of maple tree roots.

A Green Turtle Cigar tin.

"Ben!," she screamed, her hoarse screech upsetting the August afternoon. "Ben! I'm here!"

Someone struggled to close an upstairs window in the house. Voices argued.

"My Katie!" drifted and ebbed from above.

An outline of a little face at the window, pounding, pounding on the glass.

"Miss Penton."

Mr. Milos stood next to her like an oak tree, arms reaching for her.

"Ben," she turned to Mr. Milos as if she urgently needed to explain something to him. Grasped at him with one hand, her open mouth striving to speak but all she could manage was a feeble, "Ben's here."

"You're hurt, Miss. I need to get you home to your mama."

"I'm…"

The haze about her mutated to a deep purple. Black. Mr. Milos caught her in his arms.

Ben and Fireflies

It wasn't the way fireflies sputtered and flashed through a summer's eve like tiny Tinker Bells that enthralled Ben.

He didn't chase or try to capture them in a Mason jar the way the twins did. Never would Ben imprison a living thing.

Although Ben appreciated their beauty, it was after Papa told him about the brief lifespan of a firefly and how they lit up the night and danced as a way of attracting a mate that Ben watched them with great intensity. Kate thought he looked like a statue. He barely moved as he sat on the porch witnessing the sparkling splendor across the grass.

"Like they can only dance one time, and it has to be their very bestest," Ben observed.

20

Ben Gone 92 Days
Sunday, August 23, 1931

Ben's garden withered in the late August sun like fireflies trapped in a Mason jar.

Corn stalks, once six feet tall and green, had collapsed into skinny, parched versions of their best days in the sun. Rabbits and deer shared browning lettuce remnants beneath Ben's smiling scarecrow. His sunflowers, sad and thirsty, had closed and bent to avoid the sun they had once raced one another to reach.

A breeze puffed dust from the rows of weeds.

Tommy had seen Kate trying to weed Ben's garden and shooed her away to the porch, telling Mémère, who kept her beady eyes on Kate thereafter.

So Kate rocked. That's all she had done since arriving home two days ago. She hurt and rocked in Mémère's white rocking chair on the porch. One eye boasted yellow and purple while her ribs ached with every breath.

Her right arm never stopped throbbing. Broken in two places, Dr. Smythe had claimed. Maybe never to heal properly. Time would tell. Wrapped in a white plaster of Paris cast, it hung limp and useless in a red cloth sling.

She rocked. Watched Ben's garden brimming with weeds and dust. She rocked and ached in the hazy, still days that spoke of autumn. Listened to the even soar of cricket song, the cacophony of squirrel chatter. Watched crows gather and squawk along the wood's edge.

Ben had heard her. He'd called to her from the window of the castle-like house.

Mr. Milos knew some people in Traverse City, and they had been able to arrange for a telegram to be sent to Mama by way of Dr. Smythe. Mr. Milos knew of Doctor Smythe from when Mama had called the doctor out to tend to Edgar's leg.

What goes around comes around as Mémère liked to say.

After spending one night with the Milos family by the tracks in Traverse City awaiting her ride home, Kate was haunted by her thoughts. The Milos family was so poor. But they were still together. A family. Would it be better if her family lived that way? At least she would be with Ben.

Mr. Milos had told her how he had known it was her on the train but didn't want to let others know she was a girl. He knew the kind of trouble that could cause. He planned on talking to her as soon as they reached Traverse City, but she took off so fast. He found her when the teens were attacking her. He'd yelled at them and beat at them with a stick. Another man helped, but by the time they had dispersed the teens, Kate was gone.

After what her mother had done for his family, Mr. Milos said he couldn't let Kate wander about Traverse City hurt and alone.

She'd woken in the freight yard with the Milos family. Frantic, she'd tried to get Mr. Milos to let her go back for Ben or to bring Ben there. He refused, saying if this is where her mama wanted Ben, then it must be for the best.

Kate envisioned the Samuelson's castle house with the golden turrets. The swing in the beautifully groomed yard.

And the thin, quiet Milos boy, living in train yards, filthy, hurting and hungry every day of his life.

Riding home, hurting beyond all reason, Kate had been wedged between Tommy and Dr. Smythe, who had driven up to get her.

But she hadn't cried. Crying never did any good.

Tommy informed Kate that Mémère's gold pocket watch had been bartered to Doctor Smythe for her care.

Mama had sold her hand-painted tea set to pay for gas to Traverse City and back.

He thought Kate should know.

Ben Cooks

Although Ben was picky about what he ate, he loved to help in the kitchen.

Mama would ask Ben to bring her items from the icebox or cupboard and place them on the counter. This he did.

He would place one egg on the counter, making sure it stayed in its place. Then he would collect the next requested item and place it next to the egg. So it would continue, item after item, until everything Mama had asked for sat in a row, equal distances apart, like good little soldiers.

If Mama used the vanilla before the baking soda when the baking soda had been placed before the vanilla on the counter, Ben would move everything over so there was no empty space.

Ben didn't like empty spaces.

Ben liked order.

21

Ben Gone 94 Days
Tuesday, August 25, 1931

Kate didn't mean to find it. She wasn't looking for it. Although it had never been far from her thoughts.

She had been trying to help by emptying the twin's narrow bedroom closet. Although she couldn't fold with only one good hand, she could remove clothes with her left and place them on the bed for Mama to sort through. It was impossible to just sit anymore. The pain had become normal for her.

Mama had said the bank would take possession of the farm the first week of September. She hadn't signed the papers yet but expected the men in suits any day now. Kate almost smiled as she pictured her mother signing her flowery signature with a flourish as if she was the great movie star Gloria Swanson herself.

The twins would be leaving in a few days. First Raymond to Ontario, Canada, then Leo to Boston soon after.

Never since birth had they spent more than an hour apart. Now they were to live in different countries. Kate was doomed to live on a farm as a housemaid for her mother's cousins' family by early September. Once the bank took possession of the farm, Mémère, Mama, and Tommy would room at the boarding house until it was time for Tommy to leave.

Kate stopped to listen. From somewhere near the barn Raymond was yelling at Leo, Leo laughing and antagonizing his twin. She stored the sounds of their arguing voices in a mental strongbox.

That's when she saw it.

Poking out from underneath a pile of clothes on the closet floor. A plain brown paper package. It bore no labels or markings and seemed much smaller than she had envisioned it all the time she had searched for it.

Since her birthday last February.

Grasping it as best she could in her left hand, Kate carried it to Leo's bed. She set it down on top of a pile of clothes.

She had no reason to believe it was what she thought it was. It was just a brown parcel tied with string. No ribbons or lace. Not pink.

Sitting on the bed next to the parcel she studied it. The thought of Papa buying her this dress for her birthday coursed warm through her bones. She closed her eyes with the thrilling joy of it.

She was Papa's princess, ever and always. That would never change. He loved her still. Although she felt desperate to tear it open, she waited.

To relish such happiness.

Her sudden gasp surprised her. As did the thought: If this was her dress, then Papa hadn't been crossing Amsterdam Street that day to buy it for her.

Kate stood, then sat. The pain that surged through her had nothing to do with her injuries.

He had to have bought it before that day.

Tommy's words reverberated: *It wasn't an accident.*

Working her good hand under the string, she pulled it taught; it released. The brown parcel paper opened with little effort.

How Ben Talked

Ben was never much of a talker.

Kate had spoken in complete sentences at the age of two. Tommy and the twins by the time they were two and a half. Ben spoke by that age, but Kate was the only one who could understand him.

Mémère worried about his inability to speak. Since he had been named after her favorite brother, Benoit, who died at the age of fourteen from typhoid, Mémère took Ben's intelligence personally.

Raisins were "yat yahs" and toast was "phee." Since Kate spent the most time with Ben, she was the one who interpreted his words for the grownups. Rarely did he say more than one word at a time, and it sounded like a language all his own.

One day when Ben was three years and four months old, he was sitting at the breakfast table, Kate buttering his "phee" for him.

He studied his fingers and then his naked toes with great interest before asking, "Why are my toes so much smaller than my fingers?"

Kate figured Ben hadn't spoken much until he had something worth saying.

22

She knew the second the brown paper unfolded.

No Lucerne Blue peeked from within. Stroking the material confirmed it was not crepe either. It was cotton like all her other dresses.

Orange and brown cotton.

In a plaid pattern similar to a dress she had worn when she was eight years old.

Kate stretched the dress across the pile of clothes on the bed.

It was too small. She could tell just by looking at it.

Scrambling, she searched the packet for a card or a note. Something from Papa explaining why he had bought her this dress.

The price tag dangling from one sleeve confirmed it had cost considerably less than her cherished $16.75 *Good Housekeeping* dress.

No nylons.

"Kate," came from the bottom of the stairs.

Here was her dress. Her birthday dress. The dress of her dreams that was supposed to be a beautiful Lucerne blue, Paris-inspired crepe dress Papa was going to buy her because she was his princess.

"Katherine."

She wouldn't cry. Crying never did any good.

Grabbing the dress by its rough collar, she tossed it onto the floor, raised her foot above it, preparing to stomp the mundane pumpkin colored cloth.

She stared at it for several seconds, foot poised.

Lowering her leg slowly, she gathered the dress from the floor. Carefully, she smoothed its limp skirt across the bed, folding it as best she could. "Coming, Mama."

Ben Gone 97 Days
Wednesday, August 26, 1931

The house remained a stronghold of busyness with Mama and Mémère washing and mending everyone's clothes, packing for the twins, and sorting through their possessions. What little they would be able to take with them living at the boarding house. The Vanderveldes would store in their barn the few boxes Mama and Mémère couldn't take with them.

Boxes and crates filled the parlor and dining room, the kitchen counter and table piled high with clean, folded clothes. Mémère spent most of her days rocking on the front porch mending pants, shirts and underwear.

An amber haze yawned along the horizon promising another steamy August day. As air thickened with the pungent aromas of brushfires, gray white smoke lingering like a lonesome ghost in the distance, Mama washed windows. Awakened early by her throbbing arm, Kate rocked at the far end of the porch, watching Mama.

Why? wondered Kate. With all Mama had to do to get herself and everyone else ready to leave. With the bank taking over the farmhouse and land as it stood. Why did she bother to wash the windows?

Kate watched a narrow lemon-colored leaf meander

        —zig

    —zag

          —almost

            —there

              —to the grass.

Tent worms had infiltrated the black walnut trees, creating the wispy webs Kate hated and Ben admired. Bees and butterflies performed a delicate ballet about red and purple zinnias alongside the barn. Kate inhaled the spicy warm scent of rotten crabapples dropped sporadically along the drive. Summer wildflowers, white, gold, yellow, and purple, thrived stiff and stubborn along the wood's edge.

All for Ben.

At first she had been alone.

After their supper of vegetable stew and bread, Kate had sneaked away from the hustle and bustle of the house and chores.

To Ben's garden.

Shade enveloped the garden earlier every evening now.

Kneeling took a bit of time, but she did it. She had to sit back on her heels for balance. Starting along the nearest row, she pulled one weed after another with her left hand.

The small pile of stones she'd set aside for Ben weeks ago remained.

Her body complained after just five minutes, but she continued. She had no idea how she would be able to water the garden, knowing she couldn't pump the windmill well or wield the bucket to fill it. But she would do it. Somehow.

She'd promised Ben.

With every plop of a forlorn weed beside her, she felt purpose.

Someday she would be with her Ben again. Someday they would be a family again. Deep within her aching bones she knew it.

Just as deep within she knew the truth about Papa.

A shadow fell, and Tommy now worked next to her. He'd simply knelt, nodded, and starting pulling weeds without a word. He clipped along at a strong pace, his pile of weeds three times higher than hers.

"Look out," Raymond warned, appearing out of nowhere.

He sprinkled along one row from his big green watering can.

"I was going to do that!" Leo exploded from behind.

"Leo, why don't you get the hoe and start over at that end," Tommy directed, pointing to the opposite end of the garden.

Grumbling as he dragged his feet to the shed, Leo did as he was told.

Tommy threw ripe vegetables to one side, overripe or rotten to another.

Brothers and sister worked for almost an hour in wordless unison. Hoeing, weeding, watering, tending Ben's garden.

Mama watched from the porch for a few minutes. Then went back inside.

Kate fully expected her to call them to other chores. There was so much that had to be done preparing to leave. The garden would stay behind.

Halting, she ignored the pain pounding through her.

Instead she listened to the Ben song thrumming within her. Bluejays chattered and a rabbit hopped along the edge of the woods, displeased at these humans in the garden.

Suddenly Kate understood why Mama had washed the farmhouse windows that morning.

Mama washed the windows as a matter of pride. The house was still hers. Nobody had taken it from her. Not yet.

She washed the windows because she could.

This patch of dry, weed-ridden dirt was Ben's garden.

The garden was important to Ben.

So the garden was important to them.

They tended Ben's garden because Ben couldn't.

Ben's Christmas Gift

Weeks before Christmas, Ben's siblings poured over the Sears and Roebuck catalog, folding pages, circling and initialing their choices for Papa to send to Santa Claus.

Kate sat with Ben, turning page after page filled with pictures of wagons and games and trucks and clothes. But Ben didn't want any of those things.

Ben wanted snowflakes. Not just a few snowflakes, but hundreds of snowflakes. It wasn't a matter of wanting it to snow. They almost always had snow on the ground at Christmas time.

Ben wanted his own snowflakes.

So Kate stole a thick sheath of paper Papa often brought home from work for Ben to draw on. After bribing the twins with illicit food, bartering chores with Tommy, and promising Mémère to confess her multitude of sins for a month, Kate had Ben's gift.

When Ben opened a red-bowed box on Christmas morning, he giggled with delight before pouring the hundreds of white paper snowflakes over his head.

23

Ben Gone 99 Days
Sunday, August 30, 1931

Kate heard automobile tires crackling down the drive.

She didn't look up from wiping down the porch pillars. It seemed futile cleaning the pillars with the constant dust.

Yet she cleaned them.

She didn't look up when the car stopped in front of the porch.

Kate didn't want to see the bankers in their black automobiles and black suits which reflected their black hearts.

Her family hadn't attended church this morning as there was no money for gas. Mémère hadn't said a word. Usually she whined and complained in French, tatted like a mad woman, at missing her Sunday Mass. Not today.

When the dust from the automobile finally settled, Kate peeked.

A trim man about Papa's age was wearing a threadbare navy suit, too heavy a material for summer. He sported a skimmer straw hat and a pencil thin mustache. Removing his hat revealed a sunburned scalp. Hair the same daffodil yellow as his mustache fringed above his ears. Neatly manicured hands twirled the hat brim in one constant motion. Dark spread along his starched collar.

"Good afternoon, Miss," he said with a gentlemanly lilt. "Might your mother be home?"

He didn't look like the auction bankers to Kate. Maybe he was just one of the many door-to-door salesmen who both-

110

ered them on a weekly basis. He didn't carry a portmanteau of any kind. Just the same, her stomach went sour.

She started to twirl her hair, then stopped herself.

"May I tell her who is calling?" Kate asked in as polite a voice as she could muster.

The man stared at her red sling, the fading purple and mustard colored bruise on her face. Not having seen many people since returning from Traverse City, Kate felt her face glow hot.

"Are you...Miss Kate Penton?" the man asked.

Kate said yes and excused herself to find Mama.

Spying through the parlor curtains, Kate saw Mama greet the man in her usual polite fashion, her smile bright above her thin, baggy shift. She offered him a rocking chair on the shady porch and a cold lemonade, apologizing for not having cookies or cake readily available for his visit.

"Not at all, not at all, Mrs. Penton." A creak escaped the chair as it rocked forward with his words.

He stuttered and sweat profusely.

"Mrs. Pen...Penton, first, allow me to express my condolences on the...the passing of Simon...Mr. Pen...Penton."

Mama smiled and thanked him. Cardinals chirped, one near, one far.

"Mrs. Penton," the man whispered hoarsely. He cleared his throat twice. "My name is Carl Montgomery. I worked with your late husband at the bank."

Retrieving a folded white handkerchief from his breast pocket, Mr. Montgomery wiped the sweat beads from his brow and dabbed at his neck. He sipped the lemonade and cleared his throat once more. Kate sensed his nervousness the same way Mémère sensed the presence of sin.

"I attended Simon's funeral..."

"I believe I recall you there. It was kind of you to come," Mama said with quiet grace.

"Mrs. Penton." He breathed as deeply as a human might, exhaling at a slow, even pace, as if to steady himself. His round pale-lashed eyes locked onto hers. "This is more than a social call."

Hands folded on her lap, Mama waited. The afternoon air moved slower than a wounded turtle.

Mr. Montgomery withdrew a heavy looking brown envelope from his inside breast pocket. The envelope shook within his grasp as he spoke.

"Mrs. Penton. It is with great humility and regret I must admit…that I am unworthy of Simon's friendship. Or of your kind…kindness."

Kate watched Mama's head tilt, her mouth loll open with confusion.

"Please, allow me to speak without interruption." His right palm stayed Mama's words. "This is…the most difficult thing I've…Simon was a good friend to me. I was aware of his…financial difficulties. He didn't share much with me but…I knew. I also knew…"

He straightened his back, squeezing and unsqueezing his mouth before continuing.

"This was meant for you."

He handed the envelope to Mama.

"I assure you, Madam, every penny is accounted for."

With his nod, Mama lifted the envelope flap.

"I must admit to…losing many a night's slumber, tempted to use it for my own means." He swabbed his upper lip with the handkerchief. "Simon had a life insurance policy. He cashed it in the day before…" Mr. Montgomery paused before speaking with great deliberation. "He knew the policy wouldn't pay out if cause of death was…at all suspicious." His words rushed over his tongue like a toxic waterfall. "He gave the insurance money to me that day and bade me give it to his wife and children should anything happen to him. He knew there wasn't enough to pay what was owed on the farm and his incurred debt at the bank both. If the monies he'd borrowed from the bank were discovered…and I swear, Mrs. Penton, he truly did intend on repaying the monies…he knew he would be incarcerated. No doubt that's why he…"

Kate swallowed nothing in her desert dry mouth. It was several minutes before Mama spoke.

"Why now, Mr. Montgomery? I don't…"

"I was a coward!" His bellow reverberated throughout the barn and house, causing Kate to jump back from the open parlor window.

"I beg your pardon, Madam," his voice softened with apology, "…but…I brought the money to the funeral," he spoke through tense lips. "I meant to give it to you then but…I lost my position with the bank. I have a family too."

Kate watched as Mama touched the money in the envelope as if it might siphon blood from her fingertips.

Mr. Montgomery's face started to crumple before regaining its pink composure.

"When I read about the auction of your farm, I…I meant to bring it to you then. It was when I heard about Simon's little girl…what she went through, getting hurt and all…running away…"

His eyes brimmed.

"That little girl…I met her out front…she was Simon's princess. He doted on her. If I had given you the monies when I was supposed to…"

Tommy stood beside Kate, who held a finger to her lips.

Mr. Montgomery sloshed down the rest of his lemonade, settled the empty glass on the side table, and stood.

He spoke in the stilted manner of an unrehearsed actor in a stage play.

"Simon was a good friend. I will miss his laughter."

After tipping his hat to Mama, he trotted down the porch steps to his automobile and disappeared in a cloud of dirt.

How Ben Could Wait

Once Kate had begged Mama to buy her a pink hair ribbon.

Mama said Kate needed another hair ribbon like she needed cake for breakfast. She said Kate's hair was too short to wear ribbons anyway.

None of that mattered to Ben. He wanted Kate to have her hair ribbon.

Ben offered to gather eggs for a penny when it was the twins' turn. They didn't pay him. Once Mémère discovered they weren't doing their own chores, she paid Ben his penny and assigned a penance to Raymond and Leo that involved confession for three Sundays running.

Tommy had promised Ben he would play catch with him, then said he had homework to do. Since so much of his homework was math problems, Ben offered to do them for a penny.

He drew a picture of their house and of their horse, Mr. Big, which brought Papa's praise and a penny.

When he had earned enough pennies, Ben promised Tommy if he would go into the Mercantile in town to buy Kate's ribbon, he would do Tommy's math homework for the next week for free.

All this Ben accomplished with great economy of words when barely five.

Six weeks after Kate had begged for her pink hair ribbon, and possibly forgotten about it altogether, Ben presented it to her.

24

Kate cared about the money with the same fervor as Ben avoided meat.

Mama had signed the papers for the Samuelsons to legally adopt Ben before Kate had run away to Traverse City. She hadn't wanted Kate to know, fearful of what her daughter might do. Kate decided it wouldn't have made any difference had she known.

The Samuelsons had moved to create more of a distance between themselves and the Pentons.

He doesn't have a sister anymore.

Kate refused to look Mama in the eye. No matter how much Mama begged for her understanding, imploring her to see she was doing what was best for Ben, Kate ignored her.

They could pay back the bank with the monies from Mr. Montgomery. From Papa.

Nobody had to leave. They could keep the farm.

It pleased Kate to watch the twins squabble, knowing they wouldn't be parted. Tommy had an idea to start working the apple orchard like Papa had always wanted to do. They would have to create an income from the farm to pay taxes and survive within the next year. He gathered the books and half-written plans from Papa's desk and studied them. Wrote lists. Begged Kate to help him. Maybe, she said. But she didn't.

After all had been unpacked, replaced and restored within the house and farm, life went on. There was no school. The

116

cast remained on Kate's useless right arm, the red sling replaced by a white one. Her face had healed but for a soreness about her jaw when she chewed or yawned. She still struggled to sleep in comfort with her injured ribs.

August ended and September arrived, deepened, declaring autumn's imminence. Black walnuts rat-a-tatted off the barn roof like ammunition, squirrels stuffing their cheeks beyond full with their ill-gotten gains. Crimson bordered the maple leaves as a promise of grandeur to come. August smells of meadows and steamy rain were replaced with September's musty golden aura.

Wildflowers and weeds, many willowy, tangled and vibrant still from the August sun, colored the meadow with unspeakable splendor—soft heathers, mustard centered daisies, magenta and orange berries, delicately embroidered Queen Anne's lace. Survivors.

Others accepted their fate with a fond farewell, waving like summer wheat tassels in the breeze.

Kate tended Ben's garden.

She'd learned to pump the well with her left hand without spilling too much. Tommy often helped her lug the watering cans and sprinkle the garden just as Ben liked. One row, then the next. Leo and Raymond worked to harvest what they could of Ben's potatoes, corn, lettuce, and onions.

Tommy said neither he nor Mama had told them to.

Papa's Razor

Ben liked to help Papa shave in the mornings.

First, Ben would help put the water in Papa's shaving mug so he could whip it up into fluffy white cream for his face. Ben whipped it with all his might.

Papa always said that Ben was his best helper.

When Papa brushed the shaving cream across his cheeks and under his chin, he sometimes puffed a little on Ben's cheek too. Looking at the two of them side by side in the mirror, Ben wanted to laugh but was afraid of getting shaving cream in his mouth.

Sometimes Papa let Ben use a straight razor without the blade in it to shave his face. Ben did it just the way Papa did: up slowly and carefully, rinse the razor in the sink, then up slowly and carefully again until most of the shaving cream was gone.

One morning when Ben was helping Papa shave, Papa gave him his bladeless straight razor to keep. Papa seemed sad after he shaved that day. That was the day he told Ben that even if he could no longer see Papa, Papa would always be able to hear Ben sing to him.

He asked Ben to promise he would sing to him always.

Ben promised.

25

Ben Gone 117 Days
Thursday, September 17, 1931

Mama stood in front of the porch door, her daisy embroidered apron wet from the colander of freshly washed green beans clutched to her midsection as she watched the long black limousine drive up.

Mémère tatted and rocked on the porch. She spoke in French to Mama, who assured her in English all was fine. Just bank officers with more papers to sign so they could keep the farm.

Broom grasped in her left hand, Kate swept crisp apricot and brick red leaves off the porch with uneven movements.

A blue uniformed chauffeur emerged from the driver's side. Tipping his cap to Mama and Mémère, he walked behind the limousine to the back passenger door facing the porch.

Uninterested in more bankers, Kate swept a cluster of moist leaves into the bushes. The colander clattered to the porch, beans scattering. Kate watched Mama's hand cover her mouth in astonishment.

"Mon Dieu," Mémère whispered, crossing herself.

Kate heard it before she saw it. The squeak of a swinging metal handle.

Closing her eyes, she promised herself she was wrong. Prayed for the first time since Papa had died that she wasn't. Heart thudding like a thousand thunders, she tried to turn and look but couldn't make herself, frozen with doubt.

Please, Papa, please.

Slowly, as one season turns to the next, she looked.

The chauffeur held the back limousine door open. Two Buster Brown shoes attached to scrawny unscabbed legs plopped onto the drive from the back seat.

"Ben!" Tommy yelled from the barn.

Ben wore khaki shorts with suspenders, a crisp blue shirt, new socks and shiny Buster Brown shoes, the Green Turtle Cigar tin squeaking in hand.

Kate tried not to. Held her breath to stay the tears.

"Kate, I got new shoes." He pattered a Ben jig in the dirt. "See?"

Her broom clattered onto the porch. Heat burst from within her in a whelp of a cry. Then another. Collapsing onto the porch floor, she sobbed, her head dropping to her chest with each heave. Never ending tears streamed, her dress front soaked. She wept for Papa. For Mama. For herself. Gulping air, she couldn't stop the roar of redemption within from escaping in a cascade of tremulous sobs.

"Hi Mama," Ben said, stepping through strewn green beans to hug an astonished Mama around her wet waist. "They were nice people, but I wanted to come home."

As if he'd been playing at a friend's house for an afternoon.

The chauffeur piled several pieces of luggage in front of the porch steps before handing Mama an envelope.

"Mrs. Samuelson said this would explain everything, Ma'am," he said, then drove away.

Ben had crouched on his haunches to Kate's level.

He touched her sling with the gentleness of an angel saving a sinner.

"Does it hurt?" Falling to his knees, he kissed her arm.

She realized he thought she was crying because her arm hurt. But Kate no longer felt pain.

Sniffling, Mama sat on the porch steps and opened the envelope. Ben leaned on her shoulder from behind as if reading the letter too, Mama's hand resting on his as she read.

Dear Mrs. Penton:

It is with sorrow and humility that I return your son to you. The adoption papers are enclosed to destroy as you see fit.

We tried so to make Ben happy. I thought he might be happier in Traverse City, but he still missed his lake. He tried to till a garden in our backyard. He climbed trees and would not come down. Finally, after seeing your daughter from the window a few weeks ago, he refused to talk or eat. When he ran away for two nights, we knew we could not make him happy with us.

It pains my heart as I've grown to love him dearly. He is a special boy. But Ben was not meant to be ours. His heart belongs elsewhere. I am sending his clothes and toys with him.

Best Wishes,

Lillian Samuelson

Skipping towards the porch steps, Ben wiggled his fingers for his sister.

"Let's go see my garden."

She clasped his thin fingers in hers.

"Yes, Ben Boy."

Epilogue

September 2006
Ben 79
Kate 86

Slowly, Ben leaned to retrieve the fallen shawl from the porch floor. He replaced it onto Kate's fragile shoulders as she continued to rock.

She hadn't noticed its absence.

The acrid aroma of burning leaves floated across the early autumn breeze that ruffled his thick white hair, Kate's rust colored shawl.

Ben had stayed in Michigan after earning a PhD in Mechanical Engineering on academic scholarship at the University of Michigan. He'd worked as a Ford engineer for forty some years. Raised three boys with his sweet Annie he'd met at college. Raymond now lived in a retirement community in Florida near one of his sons. Tommy had died four years earlier from complications of pneumonia.

Leo had been killed in Germany during World War II.

Kate's career as a photo journalist had taken her across continents, to other worlds and then some. Yet she and Ben had always stayed in touch. Out of the blue the phone would ring at 3:00 a.m. and it would be Kate calling from somewhere in Africa or Asia. Divorced twice, she had two daughters. Samantha lived in Boston, Lilly in New Mexico. Both had offered to take Kate in once it became evident she could no longer live alone. Leaving the stove burners on or forgetting to eat.

But Ben wanted Kate with him. He'd lived alone since losing his Annie three years ago. As long as he could, he would take care of Kate.

A sly smiled creased his lips, his blue eyes, as clear as ever, simmered with quiet glee.

Yesterday Kate had commented on the lovely citrus fragrance in the bathroom. Ben told Kate she had chosen the shell-shaped air freshener herself. From within her tapestry of wrinkles, dimples had winked like twilight through trees on their lake. So many years ago.

And when she had asked again about the lovely fragrance in the bathroom after Ben fixed her bagels and fruit for breakfast this morning, Ben repeated his lie.

Just to see her smile.